CASH VALLEY

RYAN K. NELSON

ISBN 13 – 978-1540335821

ISBN – 1540335828

PART I

1

The phone rang.

It startled Agent Alex Travis as he glanced toward it, wondering how long he had been reading from the file lying open on his desk. It was late in the day. A quick peek out the window showed the long, thin shadows stretching their way down State St. from his third floor office window.

He leaned back in his chair and looked at the ringing phone with uncertainty, reluctant to be interrupted while in the middle of his work. The industrial espionage case laid out in front of him wasn't particularly compelling, he had worked plenty of similar cases, but he wanted to review it one last time to make sure he had the facts straight before starting his investigation.

After a necessary sigh, Agent Travis conceded and reached for the phone. "Agent Travis," he said, speaking with forced authority. The line was silent. He listened but heard nothing. About to hang up, he heard something, like the faint scratching of whiskers into the receiver.

"Hello?" he tried again, this time in his normal tone.

"Hello," said the voice of an older man.

"Yes?" Travis asked, irritated at the delay. "What can I do for you?"

"Yeah, I was looking for the agent in charge of the Cache County Bank robbery. Your lady who answers the phones said to wait. Do I talk to you about it?" the unknown caller asked.

Travis's irritation quickly dissipated, replaced with curiosity. He hadn't thought much about the Cache County Bank robbery lately. How long had it been, two years since the unexpected heist had garnered national attention in the fall of 1952?

Intrigued, he said, "This is Agent Travis. Now who am I speaking with?" as he reached for a pencil.

"I'm nobody. But I'm calling on behalf of somebody. Somebody who wants to talk to you," the old man answered.

"Then put 'somebody' on the line and let me talk to him," Agent Travis quipped back, his brow furrowed in puzzlement.

"Would if I could, but he ain't here."

Great, another waste of time, Travis thought. How many calls have I answered just like this one? Another dead end. He was about to hang up the phone when the voice continued.

"He said he wants to meet. Has something to tell you about the case. Come to Green Canyon in Logan. Drive till the road ends. He'll be there at 9 a.m. every day this week," the old man said, sounding as if he couldn't care less about the details that grabbed Agent Travis's full attention.

"Is that everything?" Travis asked, scribbling furiously on his pad of paper.

"That's everything." The old man's voice trailed off.

"Wait!" exclaimed Travis, but it was too late. The line went dead. Travis looked at the phone, deep in thought. He knew most cases were solved not only by the investigative work of good agents, but also by random leads given from the public, especially when cases had gone cold, like this one.

He hung up the phone and eased back in his chair, which squeaked in protest. The chair was metal with unsightly green cushions that provided little comfort. "It's not much but it will do," his supervisor had told him when he came to the Bureau four years ago. If it wasn't much then, it was even less now. Still, as a junior agent straight out of college, he didn't have much bargaining power. Four years later, he still wasn't sure he had done enough yet to warrant asking for a new one.

He stared blankly at the file on his desk, now relegated to an afterthought as he tried to recall all of the details he knew about the robbery case. The $300,000 take wasn't overly astounding given the Great Brinks Robbery of 1950 in Boston, Massachusetts, just two years prior. That heist netted the robbers over $1.2 million in cash and $1.5 million in checks and money orders – the largest robbery in United States history at the time.

But that was Boston. For little Logan, Utah, nestled in the quiet northeast corner of the state, it had rocked the foundation of the community, and the federal government took notice. If crimes of this magnitude could happen in Logan, then nowhere in America was safe.

Still reeling from their inability to solve the Great Brinks robbery, the FBI had resolved to make quick work of this case to show the country that robbing a federal institution was bad business. But when the original head agent, a Salt Lake office star named Bower, ran out of leads after only six months, the finger pointing began. No one wanted to own the result. Ultimately, his supervisors panicked and granted him permission to transfer to the Los Angeles field office so he could save face and they could start again.

Next to take over the case—a veteran agent named Smith with twenty years of experience. Agent Travis had liked his calm demeanor. Smith proceeded with a more even keel. He wasn't one to engage in the egotistical behavior that often prevailed in an office filled with men bent on being heroes. Travis had a similar style and took the opportunity to learn from him whenever he had the chance.

Smith had started over at the beginning, re-interviewing witnesses, viewing photos, searching for evidence – but in the end came no closer to solving the case than Agent Bower. Now thirteen months after the robbery, the case had gone cold and unfortunately, so had Smith. Apparently, while celebrating his 49th birthday at home with his family, he'd dropped dead from a heart attack.

It came as a considerable shock the next morning when Travis heard the news. Smith was here one day and gone the next, just like the money at Cache County Bank, which now seemed even more likely to be gone for good.

It took all of an hour that morning after Smith's death before Agent Travis found himself being called into his supervisor's office. Agent Tom Anderson was the Special Agent in Charge for the Salt Lake field office. He was a tall and lanky man, known for his no-nonsense approach to his work, requiring that of everyone else in the office as well.

"Travis, this isn't easy," Agent Anderson started. "We all miss Smith."

Travis watched him closely, as the morning light slipped through the half open blinds, the dust dancing mindlessly in its rays. Travis sat patiently, his investigative skills telling him his boss was already through mourning and wanted the quickest path to get everyone back to work.

"But justice doesn't stop when a man goes down," he continued, trying to sound patriotic. It didn't work. "Right now the best way we can remember him is to push forward, finish what he started. It's what Smith would have wanted."

Agent Travis moved his hand up over his mouth and lightly thumbed at his lip, not sure exactly how to respond to that. He kept a concerned look and waited for his boss to get to the point.

"That's why I am assigning you the Cache County Bank robbery," he said finally, as he dropped the large file on his desk in front of Agent Travis. "You know the story so I won't repeat it. The notes from Bower and Smith are inside. I'm giving you a lot of leeway on this one. You will have access to all the resources you need so make us proud."

Agent Travis stared at the file on the desk. That's how it works, he thought, once the opportunity for glory fades. Now it's all about who will get stuck with it. Naturally, the obvious candidates are the incompetent, the burned out, or, in Agent Travis's case, the new guy. It all added up. Eventually every agent is given that one chance to earn a respectable reputation, or become part of the future group of incompetents.

"It's not waiting to shake hands with you. Pick it up and get out," Agent Anderson said impatiently as he pointed to the door.

Travis looked up, embarrassed. "Yes sir." He got up and reached for the file, still trying to decide if this was a blessing or a curse.

As he closed the door behind him, he tucked the file tightly under his arm, and headed back to his desk. It didn't take a room full of FBI agents to figure out what had just happened. As he walked, he glanced at the faces of his co-workers, each showing a varying level of interest but none lasting more than a moment. A case changing hands wasn't at the top of the list for excitement in a place like this.

Once back at his desk, he positioned the file in front of him, unopened, and leaned back in his chair. A faint smile formed on his lips. Despite the presumption that he was only getting the case because it had become toxic for the other agents that had a reputation to protect, Agent Travis was glad to have something above the menial cases he was commonly assigned. Most of those cases dealt with financial crimes, like fraud and embezzlement. That kind of work, while essential, barely required him to carry a weapon. It was primarily based on research, obtaining warrants and making arrests of white collar criminals at their place of business, usually while they cried like babies.

With this case, Agent Travis saw an opportunity, a challenge, which was the exact reason he joined the FBI in the first place. He had a knack for details, but played things close to the vest, not wanting to be like many of the other narcissistic Agents. His motivation was a belief that right and wrong still existed, and getting it right mattered.

But there was one problem that lingered in the back of his mind—Bower and Smith were competent agents, and they had come up empty. He would need to focus on working a different angle, to see the things they missed, a daunting task given their level of expertise and experience. For this, Agent Travis needed time to think, time to work over the details in his mind, like suspects, getting them to tell him what they know.

He had spent all of that first day diving into the evidence, mentally immersing himself in it. He memorized facts, names, the accounts of the witnesses, you name it. He hadn't let any roadblock deter him. He had worked long hours that turned into long weeks, and it wasn't long before Travis had begun to feel the weight of failing to make progress. So as had happened twice already, despite his best efforts, the case had come no closer to being solved.

Eventually, he turned his attention back to other cases, like the one that rested on his desk in front of him nearly one year later. It was a case of a man selling company trade secrets to a competitor. It felt small in comparison to the bank robbery. As he stared at it now, he already knew how it would end, with a grown man sobbing in front of his coworkers as he escorted him from the building in handcuffs.

It was then that Agent Travis resolved to make the most of this new opportunity. He arose in defiance to the still air around him and flipped the case file closed. His unsightly chair swung around in a circle as he grabbed his suit coat off the back of it and headed out the door for home thinking about only one thing…what he would find tomorrow morning at the top of Green Canyon.

2

Agent Travis awoke early, anxious to be on the road by 7 a.m. for the 97-mile drive from his home in Salt Lake to the east bench of Logan. His wife, Sarah, was up with him to make breakfast and pack him a lunch. He could have done it himself, and preferred that she sleep in given her current state, but she insisted. It was her way and she wasn't about to let the last month of her pregnancy stop her now.

"Why do you have to go to Logan today?" she asked as she brought their breakfast to the table.

"To conduct an interview. Could be important to the bank robbery case," he replied in a manner meant to reassure her that it wasn't anything dangerous. Despite his reassuring tone, he felt her eyes making their own assessment.

"Well, be safe. It's cold and wet out there. And that drive through Sardine Canyon can be treacherous."

Looking to change the subject, he asked, "Do you know why they call it Sardine Canyon?"

She scooped a healthy portion of scrambled eggs on his plate and paused, "I guess I've never really thought about it."

"Well I have," he said as he picked around his plate with his fork. "It struck me as an odd name for Northern Utah. As it turns out there are three theories."

"And let me guess, you just had to know, didn't you?" said his wife with a sly smile.

Travis looked up, grinning back. He knew she was teasing him for his inquisitive nature. He didn't mind. He enjoyed the banter.

She sat down next to him, her auburn colored hair as scrambled as the eggs after a long night of clashing with her pillow. He had learned that she couldn't care less about how her hair looked first thing in the morning. That self-assured quality appealed to him and made her more attractive in his eyes, even when her hair rioted in protest. He decided not to comment on it, keeping it a secret for the greater good.

Travis turned back to his breakfast, stabbing away at the little yellow lumps on his plate as he continued, "Some say it was from when the early settlers came to the area in the 1850s. They apparently ate sardines from tin cans and subsequently left them on the side of the canyon trail. Over time enough cans accumulated that travelers began to refer to it as Sardine Canyon. At least that is one theory."

"Well, that's odd," Sarah said, wrinkling her nose in the process.

"I know. Another version is that the settlers found small whitefish swimming in the streams. They were able to survive year-round from the water bubbling up from springs. I guess they thought that was unusual and decided they were sardines," he said, pausing as he swallowed.

"And what's the third theory?" Sarah asked.

"The third theory is that the canyon was so narrow that it felt like being packed in like sardines when traveling through it," he said smiling at the absurdity of that one.

Sarah laughed out loud. "So which one is correct?" she asked curiously.

"They're all a little suspicious," he said. "For starters, it isn't one canyon at all, but actually three connected canyons. Box Elder Canyon is the first and runs about three miles until reaching the town of Mantua (pronounced "Mant-a-way" by the locals). From there it becomes Dry Canyon for the next several miles, ironically running past Sardine Summit, with a precipitous stretch down to Dry Lake. The final canyon is Wellsville Canyon, which drops into Cache Valley."

"Also, sardines were only packaged in Europe back in the 1850s. It would be a few more decades before sardines would be canned in the United States. If travelers did use them as provisions, those little fish had come a long way."

"As for the fish theory, well it was plausible that early settlers thought they were looking at sardines. I did find one other canyon in the U.S. with the name Sardine Canyon and, curiously, it is located just to the south in nearby Ogden. Still, whatever those fish were, they weren't sardines. Sardines live in salt water, typically in the ocean, not fresh water streams."

"So it was because the canyon is so narrow?" Sarah asked.

"Well that one has problems too. Sardine Canyon doesn't appear to be any narrower than any other canyon. If anything, it is quite wide. To qualify for a name like sardine, I would expect it to have been so tight that travelers on horses would have trouble maneuvering around each other, and that clearly isn't the case."

"I wonder which one is the truth," Sarah said. "It seems a shame not to know."

"True," he answered back. "But sometimes the truth can be hard to come by. Even with extensive research the answer isn't always clear." He drifted off as his thoughts turned back to the task ahead. He wondered what 'truth' he would confront today, the actual truth or another man's perception of the truth.

Sarah's voice, and a gentle tapping on his arm, brought him back to the present.

"And sometimes the truth is so unbelievable that we would rather make up reasons that fit better, something that we can accept," she said.

She had a good point. The truth is sometimes what we make of it.

Sarah continued, "You never know, maybe there is another version that trumps them all, and it got lost somewhere along the way. I'm sure if there is, you'll find it."

Travis looked over at her. It seemed pretty clear they weren't talking about sardines and canyons anymore. She knew him well enough to know that fish stories paled in comparison to solving the bank robbery. He chewed on his toast for a minute as he thought about what she had said.

"I better get moving," he said eventually, as he eased up and walked his plate over to the sink.

"Not so fast, Agent Travis," she said, poking fun at his eagerness to get to work.

He watched as she got up slowly from her chair, careful not to bump her protruding belly against the table. She had been so careful for eight long months, making sure their first child received the best of care.

Sarah came over and wrapped her arms around him, leaning in to press the bump from their unborn baby into him. The warm comfort of Sarah's hug tempted him to change his mind and play it safe, knowing the trip had the possibility for more peril than he had let on. Travis had thought about asking another Agent to join him for the day, but on short notice, and with no assurance this tip was even real, he decided to go alone. Plus, he wasn't sure he could stand the embarrassment if it was a hoax.

Travis held the embrace, enjoying the peaceful feeling it afforded. He liked being married. It was these moments, when their bodies melded together, that brought things into perspective. He knew his first job was to take care of his wife and their soon-to-be family. He ran his hands up and down from her lower back to her shoulders, content to stay a little longer, but as he did his eyes briefly caught a glance of his watch. 6:58 a.m. If he was going to go, it was time.

"Gotta go," he whispered softly as he began to pull away. She pulled him back in and kissed him once more, holding him extra tight, before finally letting go.

Travis reached for his things and headed for the door, one last smile to Sarah in the process.

"Call me," Sarah shouted as he left.

He raised his hand in acknowledgement as the screen door swung closed behind him. He climbed into his company-issued Ford Crestliner and threw his briefcase on top of the passenger side seat. He started its flathead V-8 engine. The car rumbled to life. He was about to put the car into reverse when he was suddenly confronted with the danger that lie ahead. Anxiously, he reached over into the briefcase and pulled out a .357 caliber Smith & Wesson handgun, standard issue for military and police. He checked to make sure it was loaded and rested it on top of the briefcase. He was now ready for the journey north.

It was 8 a.m. when Agent Travis passed by Brigham City and entered the opening of Sardine Canyon. The roads were wet so he sat up to give the drive his full attention, heeding his wife's warning to drive safe. He passed Mantua, headed over the pass at Sardine Summit, and ran head on into a thick fog, something he found very unusual for Utah. Fortunately, he had plenty of low visibility driving experience growing up in the Bay Area. He calculated his visibility at about ten yards and dropped his speed accordingly. Without much to look at, it gave him time to think about the case.

The robbery was an overnight job. Someone (or more likely, a group of people) had infiltrated the bank after hours. The bank had received a shipment of money bound for Seattle earlier that day. The armed courier, as planned, had stopped in Logan shortly after 3 p.m. and deposited the money at the Cache County Bank, which had a large, three-story branch on Main Street with six vaults. The money had been stored in the basement vault, an older version with a large door and concrete walls that were reinforced with rebar.

When the employees had left for the night, the timer had been set on the vault and alarms set on the building. Nothing was out of place. Yet despite the security measures taken, upon arrival the next morning, they found the vault had been penetrated and the money – all three hundred thousand dollars – was gone, vanished into the thin air of a cool autumn night in Cache County.

The interviews conducted with the tellers, bankers and bank manager had produced little useful information. No one at the branch was aware of the money until the day of arrival. This was a common security practice. It prevented any possibility of a rogue employee tipping off a criminal. Still each employee was methodically questioned. But in the end, their stories all checked out, as did the couriers.

Leads from local residents had come pouring in too, but nothing that stood out. Agent Travis read through it all, twice, from reports of unknown individuals passing through to tools being stolen from a hardware store to someone firing a weapon down by the marsh. It wasn't due to a shortage of tips from the public that this case wasn't being solved. It's just that none of them seemed connected. They all could have occurred on any random day in Logan.

"It doesn't make any sense," he whispered to himself, as worry rested on his face.

He continued along cautiously, glancing at his watch to confirm he was still going to make it on time, when, all of a sudden, a cow appeared out of nowhere off his right side, very near to the road. Agent Travis slammed on the brakes and put the car into a full skid. He came to a stop right along the side of the bovine. Fortunately, the cow hadn't yet moved onto the road.

Travis let out a deep sigh only to have it interrupted as a horn sounded behind him. He glanced in the rear view mirror just in time to see a pick-up truck narrowly miss him as it swerved into the left lane. It continued on past him with the driver yelling and shaking his fist in the process.

Travis turned back to the cow and scowled in frustration. The cow, however, just sat there, chewing grass, with a look that seemed to say, 'If you can't handle it, maybe you should turn back.'

Agent Travis looked away, realizing that thought had come from him, not the cow. Feeling more foolish than anything, he wondered if the allure of solving a case that eluded the best agents was propelling him to take unnecessary risk. At that particular moment, Travis thought about turning the car around and heading back.

But deep down Travis knew, with the right break, he could solve this case. He didn't yet know how but he knew it was out there, somewhere hidden beneath the fog, waiting to be brought to light. It wasn't time to turn back.

His eyes focused forward as he released the brake pedal and began slowly moving ahead. As he drove past the cow, he sarcastically gave it an imaginary tip of the cap, glad the situation hadn't been worse.

After a few miles he began a steady descent that brought him under the fog line and into a glorious view of the Cache Valley. This was his favorite part of the journey. If ever there was a beautiful and serene place on earth, this was it.

Nestled between the mountains was a picturesque valley running north to south, full of vibrant colors, with the county's farming footprint laid out before him. It was a simple place, yet the valley's grandeur took on a sort of nobility that set it apart from any other he had seen. He marveled that it sat isolated in the top of the Utah Mountains, its beauty unbeknownst to most of the world. In just the short view the road had afforded him, he felt at peace, and wondered how a crime of this magnitude could co-exist with the serenity of this valley.

Agent Travis turned his attention away from the scenic view and back to reality. The few buildings that lined Main Street in the distance were visible several miles out. Not far past that would be Logan Canyon, where the road ran east to Bear Lake, and just a mile north of that was his destination, Green Canyon. It wouldn't be long now.

His mind began to focus, running through the questions he would ask and how he would ask them. His hand subconsciously drifted over to the revolver lying next to him. He picked it up and holstered it inside his suit coat.

He drew a deep breath that ended with a slow exhale and the words, "Of course, none of this matters unless that 'someone' is waiting for me at the top of Green Canyon."

3

Jack walked along the trail at a brisk pace hoping to arrive at the meeting place ahead of any possible FBI personnel that might have responded to the message. He strained to get enough air as the chill from the cool September air penetrated into his lungs. Jack knew his body was still adjusting to the altitude and temperature after his extended stay in St. George. That excursion had left him with few positive memories and he was glad to be back in Cache Valley. Despite his troubles, this was home.

He could see his destination just ahead as the trees began to part. It was the end of the road at the top of the canyon. He approached through the woods from the east. As he arrived, he cautiously looked around, making sure he was alone. He could see in the distance where the road ended and the trailhead began. He sat down on the ground, just inside the tree line, and leaned back against a rock where rays from the sun would hit his back, a trick he had learned from the geckos down south. No matter the temperature, they would always come out to the rocks to warm up in the sun, the difference being they did so without a care in the world. He felt the warmth begin to penetrate through his denim jacket, a welcome companion. His breathing soon returned to a normal state.

Today marked the second morning he had made the hike to wait for a visitor that he didn't know whether or not was coming. It was this past Saturday when Jack had met the old man who was out on the hunt. After an extended chat about deer, antelope and elk, with Jack providing some valuable tips on the best places to find them, he had decided this was the man to ask. Jack had already determined the best way forward was to get help, but he couldn't just openly stroll into town, at least not yet. He needed a messenger. And despite his reluctance to include another innocent person, he had no choice.

Fortunately, after a long pause while the stranger looked earnestly at Jack, likely seeing the desperation in the young man's eyes, he agreed to make the call. "One call, that's it," the old man said while holding his index finger up in the air before turning to walk away. Jack had breathed a sigh of relief once he was out of sight. It was the first time in a long time he had felt something close to hope.

But as Jack sat there now, warming in the morning sun, the worry had returned. It was all too possible that message was never delivered. And if it was, it was just as likely that no one would come. Still he had no choice but to wait it out every day this week as he had said, with nothing to do but fill his mind with thoughts, something Jack had become accustomed to during his time in jail. He had spent much of that time living in the memories of the past, which gave him access to better views than his cramped cell allowed. Now as Jack sat there, sun on his back, hat down low across his forehead and arms folded across his chest, he stepped back inside his mind to his former life in Cache Valley.

The common theme throughout all of his memories was this land. Until recently he had known nothing else. Born and raised in Logan, he lived a simple life. Even as World War II raged through the rest of the world, it might as well have been on another planet to him. His father was clear about what he was to do each day; chores, and school, and then more chores. That's how it was laid out. But what he did after his chores were done was up to him.

Living on the east side of Logan gave him easy access to the canyons of the Wasatch Mountains and provided him with all the adventure he desired. Jack was never short on ideas on what to explore next, where to fish or what to hunt. In fact, as far as he was concerned, Cache Valley was the perfect place to live.

His mother had known of his love for the wilderness, and used it to instill in him a deep respect for nature, which was part of her heritage. Often times she would tell him stories about Cache. His favorite was about an Indian Chief named Sagwich who was born in 1780. At that time the land was occupied sparsely by the Shoshone Indians, who subsided on the ample herds of buffalo that formerly resided here. "But the Cache winters are harsh, with lots of snow and plunging temperatures," she would say with squinted eyes and a deepening voice that would fill Jack with fear and wonder, as it was intended.

"And when the snow started building early in the fall of 1784, and to depths that were unusually high, the Indians wisely packed up their things and left for the valleys to the west. It likely saved their lives as that winter the snows continued to pile up, higher and higher. In fact, in Salt Lake it was said to have reached a depth of fourteen feet," she would try to illustrate with her hands.

"Cache Valley would have been much worse. When the Indians returned next spring they found only a handful of buffalo still alive. With no other means to survive once the game was gone, they mostly moved on and the future settlers would comment on the strange valley filled with animal bones, likely a result of the unfathomable winter of 1784," as she would finish her story. He still remembered every word.

Jack opened his eyes and looked around. A slight breeze ruffled a few leaves from a tree, but nothing else had changed, so he closed his eyes again. Every time he did, before the memories began to play, he felt a twinge of pain. He knew he had been alone too long. The feeling, the loneliness, was getting heavier.

In these times he would often recollect the words from his mother. From his earliest days he could recall her saying, "Remember Jackie, a man's strength lies within." Over and over, she reminded him of that. Even now he could still her voice in his mind.

Jack's mind spun through topics until it landed again on those early inhabitants and their way of life, exploring the land and all its treasures both above and below the earth. He liked to think of himself as a young Jim Bridger, who first set foot in the valley in the 1820s as a member of the Rocky Mountain Fur Company, a step that would mark the beginning of settling the valley. They initially named it Willow Valley due to the plentiful number of willow trees. The group was there searching for beavers, whose skins were currently in fashion and therefore, profitable. A two pound beaver pelt could fetch as much as $2 on the west coast or up to

$7.50 in New York. Having found success in the area, they came and went for several years, often storing their skins and supplies in caches underground until they returned. It wasn't long until the valley was known as 'cache' valley and the name stuck.

That was the kind of life Jack craved. He longed for his earlier, adventurous days, with his dog Trigger by his side, looking for something new to explore. In fact, he had found Trigger during just such an excursion.

Jack had been fishing at the base of the Logan canyon when a young dog, no more than two years old, appeared on the other side of the river. It didn't make a sound, just stood there watching him. Jack watched him for a while as he fished. It had the characteristics of a German Shepherd with a long snout and dark muzzle but he wasn't as large as a full grown shepherd, and the dog held his head and his tail more like a retriever would. It was likely a mixed breed, like himself.

Jack threw the dog a fish. The dog wasted no time devouring it before sitting down quietly and waiting for more. He obviously hadn't eaten in a while so Jack obliged. By the time the sun began to set the two felt right at home together. Two mixed breed scavengers, left to their own devices, without hardly a word to say. It was easy to see they were going to make a good team. From that time on, they were nearly inseparable. That is, until late last summer when Jack had to leave in a hurry. He hadn't seen Trigger since then until last week, and that reunion was cut short by necessity. He was anxious to see him again.

Jack re-opened his eyes, this time startled by a noise. He found the source and it was nothing more than two squirrels at play. He watched them for a minute before he tilted his hat back and rubbed his eyes. From where he sat, he could see the far side of the Logan valley and the flat part of the land that turned into wetlands from the river. Even from several miles away, its beauty was stunning. He longed to be back in the valley. He was so close, but it was still out of reach.

He could tell by the sun it was nearly 9 a.m. He suddenly felt the scourge of hopelessness return. Was he going to come here every day this week only to find himself alone? If so, what would be his next move? He was running out of time and he knew it. But before he could bury himself in what-ifs, he heard it. The sound of something unnatural rose up through the canyon; a rumbling of sorts, soft at first, but growing louder with each passing second. The squirrels to his right heard it as well and had stopped to listen. Jack stayed seated, staring intently at the road that ended about a hundred yards down the mountain from him. Someone was coming.

With a bit of trepidation, Jack sat listening to the sound of the motor shift up and down as it managed the climb. His right hand lowered to rest on the revolver hanging at his side. He didn't anticipate trouble, but his history had taught him to expect it. This time he had no margin for error and he wondered if he would use it against another man if he was cornered.

Around the bend a black Ford finally appeared, followed by an entourage of dust. It drove down to the very end of the road where the engine screeched to a halt before being shut-off with a dying thud. It had obviously had a long morning already.

The car door opened and out of the vehicle stepped a man in a dark suit with a dark tie. He made a 360-degree turn as he looked around at his surroundings, before putting on a hat and closing the car door. He took a few steps forward with his head still shifting from side-to-side before stopping at the front of the car and leaning back against the grill.

Jack just sat there, watching, trying to gather an impression from this stranger. It did appear that he was waiting for someone. All indications were that he was that someone. This was it, he thought, his chance to get help. It was what he had asked for, but for some reason, he stayed put right there on the ground, knowing the man below had yet to spot him.

Finally, his nerves got the best of him, and Jack slipped behind the nearest tree when the stranger looked away. This is a bad idea, he thought, as his back rubbed against the tree's bark. After all, there was a very real possibility he could end up in handcuffs…for the third time. That won't do, he told himself. "There is no way for me to protect Kate if I get locked up again," he whispered unconsciously, deep in thought.

He looked over at the two squirrels, still at play. As he watched, he envied their carefree interactions as they bounced about in the canyon, surviving together and happier for it. It reminded him of how he and Kate were when they were younger, always at play in the canyon.

It was then that Jack remembered why he was willing to take this risk in the first place. It was for Kate and it had to be done. If he ended up in jail for the rest of his life but saved hers in the process, it would be worth it.

A gust of wind placed the cool sting of the air on his face. He drew in a deep breath and stepped out from behind the tree to begin his short journey down the hill. He watched the man below as his head turned in Jack's direction. He had been spotted. There would be no going back now. He continued on his path, taking him directly west towards Logan.

Or in other words, he was headed towards home.

4

"This must be that somebody," Agent Travis said softly as he watched the stranger walking towards him in a deliberate manner.

Agent Travis watched him closely, taking in as many details as he could. He was a younger man, maybe 6' 1" to 6' 2" in height, thin but athletic build and, unless Travis was mistaken, his skin had a brownish tone. Most importantly, Travis spotted the revolver hanging from his waist on the right side. He felt an urge to grab his own pistol. First draw was critical in a gun fight. But the urge gave way to reason. Agent Travis knew it was equally important to play it cool. Remember your training, he thought. Words beat bullets on most days. When it comes time to act, then be decisive.

The young man was only twenty yards away now. Agent Travis straightened up off the grill of his car. He took one step forward and faced up towards the incoming stranger, the tension rising fast and hot like the sun. He was antsy to call out, but waited until the newcomer was a little closer, not wanting to come across as over anxious. He could see his eyes now. They looked worried, which put Agent Travis more at ease. At five yards out the young man slowed to a stop, content to let Travis speak first.

"I'm Agent Travis, FBI," he said, trying to maintain his calm demeanor despite the fact his heart was beating through his chest. "I got your message. Your friend said you had some information about a bank robbery." Maybe not exactly how it goes in training, he thought, but I moved a chess piece. Let's see how he plays back.

The man in front of him paused, and even momentarily looked away, as if he was concerned he was being ambushed. Travis stayed quiet, letting him work it out. It helped him to see that his opponent was equally nervous. It didn't take long for the young man to return his gaze back on Agent Travis.

"Yeah, I have something to tell you," the young man started. "Stuff that I know that might help. I thought you might like to know it."

"What might I like to know?" Agent Travis replied.

"About the Cache County Bank robbery," he said, now keeping his eyes locked on the FBI Agent.

Agent Travis looked away and shifted slightly to give off an apathetic response. "Well I didn't come up here for the view. What's on your mind?" Travis said as he looked back up, folding his arms across his chest in the process.

Jack stumbled for his next words saying, "I know stuff."

"Yeah, you said that," Agent Travis quickly countered, slowly gaining the upper-hand. He could tell this young man, who could barely have been twenty-one years old, had a lot on his mind. This had the potential to break the case wide open, but the revolver at his side also reminded him that it had the potential to end badly so he decided to take his time.

"How about we do this?" Agent Travis said, gesturing to a few small boulders gathered together a short distance away. "Why don't we have a seat over here on these rocks and let's take it from the top." The idea seemed to resonate with the young man, whose face showed that a more relaxed approach was the right way to proceed.

They both stepped slowly over to the rocks, Agent Travis keeping the young man in front of him all the way. Travis noted how dark their shadows were on the ground. He looked up and saw there wasn't a cloud in the sky. The sun was shining down like God's interrogation light, waiting to expose either of them.

When Jack sat down and seemed ready to continue, Agent Travis said, "Why don't you start by telling me your name?"

He hesitated, clearly contemplating whether or not to answer. Eventually, he muttered out, "Jack."

Sensing the young man was not the conversational type, Travis regrouped. "Ok 'Jack', let's come back to that one."

Agent Travis paused before continuing, "So you know a little something about one of the biggest bank robberies in American history. You were right. I am interested. Let's talk about that for a while. How about we start with who did it?"

Jack shot a glance Agent Travis's way, checking to see if he was serious. Travis returned it with a smile, easing the tension.

Jack shook his head slightly, as he straightened his back and squinted into the distance, appearing like he was contemplating where to begin. Travis could see the weight of the air pressing on the young man as he prepared to part ways with whatever burden he had been carrying.

As Agent Travis was about to try again to restart the conversation, Jack started to talk, "It's not who. There was more than one. A gang of at least five. I wasn't there for the robbery so it's hard to say."

Agent Travis jumped on that one. "If you weren't there, then how do you know?" he said, now sounding more like a lawyer than an investigator.

"You see, I'm from Logan. I was born here. I grew up not far from this canyon. I've spent my whole life in these mountains," he said as he pointed around him. "Until recently, that is," as his voice trailed off. Jack paused to flick an assassin bug that had landed on his leg before continuing, "But now I'm back. I want to square things. I can lead you to the men who stole that money, but I will need your help to protect someone."

"Who?" Agent Travis said, making mental notes of the conversation.

"There's a girl. She lives not far from here. Her name is Kate and I think she is in danger. These men are coming for her. They think she knows about the robbery," Jack said.

"Does she? Does she know?" Agent Travis said, relieved to hear that there was another person to corroborate this information.

"She knows," Jack said with his eyes staring off in the distance.

"How does she know? How do both of you know?" Agent Travis asked directly, hoping for a faster pace to the responses from the young man. He knew a slow response was more likely to be made up than a fast one. The truth doesn't need fact checking before it parts the lips, he liked to say.

"It was a couple days after the robbery, maybe two. Kate and I went up into Birch Canyon, just to the north of us, not far from here, and looped around into the back of Green Canyon. There was nothing unusual about that day to us. We spent a lot of time together up here; riding horses, exploring caves, and such. For years, Green Canyon was our playground. But as we got older, it was harder to get away with work and all. We hadn't been up here together for a while so we planned to spend the day together, exploring some of our favorite spots," Jack said.

"We knew about the robbery, everyone was talking about it, but up here, in the mountains, it didn't mean anything to us and we weren't thinking about it. That is until we came around a bend and nearly ran into a man relieving himself in the bushes. That's when it all started."

"When what started?" Travis asked.

"A bad dream really," Jack said pointedly before continuing. "We were all startled, him and us, maybe him the most. He put a gun on us right quick. I had a gun too but figured it was just an awkward situation that would soon pass. I was wrong."

"What did he look like?" Agent Travis asked, eager to get the hard facts to build a physical description of the alleged suspect.

"Rough looking, heavy…ugly," Jack said, nodding his head, content with the description. "Oh, and he smelled."

Agent Travis sat with his mouth half open at the vague description, wondering if this kid was for real. "What about a shirt, a hat…pants?" Travis asked with an extra hint of sarcasm as he stared wide-eyed over at Jack.

"Yes, all of that," Jack answered, straight-faced.

"Ok," Travis drew out slowly in disbelief. Deciding it was best to keep him talking for now, he continued on, "Tell me what happened next."

"He cursed up a storm, but in a hushed manner, looking around to see if anyone else was coming. When he was done cursing, he gave us a real nasty sort of look. Neither of us had said a word but then Kate apologized for surprising him. I think she was hoping that would get him to lower the gun, but he didn't. Instead, he cocked the hammer and extended his arm, pointing the gun right in her face, at point blank range, and saying 'you shut your mouth, doll, unless I ask you a question' or something like that," the young man said before pausing for a lengthy breath.

His hands fidgeting, he soon continued. "I didn't care for that so I stepped over in front of the gun, moving her back slightly. The man eagerly switched the muzzle to my face. He looked agitated. I thought he might pull the trigger. There wasn't much I could do. If I draw on him then, I am a dead man now."

“So how did you get out of it?” Agent Travis inquired, becoming intrigued by the story.

“We didn’t,” the young man said, emphasizing the ‘we’. My dog, Trigger, came running around the corner, nearly crashed into us. He doesn’t bark often and none of us heard him coming. The man took the gun off me and pointed it at my dog, muttering some more swear words under his breath before saying, ‘who else you got coming around the corner?’ Kate told him no one, just us. But he didn’t trust us. He told me to slowly unstrap my belt and lower it to the ground, keeping my hands off my gun. I did – had no choice. Once he had my holster he ordered us to start walking, in the direction we had originally been heading. I remember looking at Kate at that point. She had a scared look on her face. From more than what had just happened. She seemed scared for what was about to happen.”

“Then what?” Agent Travis said smoothly, urging him to keep going.

“Then he kicked my dog,” Jack said with a tinge of disgust in his voice. “Kicked him hard. He was following us and this man didn’t like that so he gave him a big kick in the hind leg. Trigger slid off into the brush with a yelp I’ve never heard from him before. I caught it all out of the corner of my eye but when I stopped to turn around I got a barrel between my shoulders. The man reached around and grabbed my throat and said, ‘don’t worry, I will come back and give it a proper burial.’ It was then I realized Kate was right. Things were going to get a lot worse.”

Jack wiped his now sweaty hands on his jeans. Travis could tell he was still uncomfortable, fidgeting, always looking around, but it didn’t take another prompt this time for Jack to continue.

“He marched us off the trail through the trees. Kate held my hand tight as we walked. I could see immediately where he was taking us. There is an old abandoned log home against the mountain. It was small. No one had lived there for a long while. It was owned by a mining company that used it to house some of the men who worked in the mines, but that was forty years ago. Mother Nature owns it now. I have been in it a lot over the years. It was a good place to stop for some shade and have lunch, maybe take a nap on the old bunks but that’s all. Most people have forgotten it’s still there, or have assumed it has fallen down.”

Then Travis noticed Jack’s demeanor change as he paused again.

When he spoke next his voice was lower and his speech even more tentative.

"I was trying to figure a way out of this, but as soon as we stepped inside he shoved me to the wall and pinned me against it. He must weigh three hundred pounds because I couldn't even breathe. He pulled out handcuffs and cuffed my right hand to an old iron stove that was bolted to the floor. Seeing that he had me all locked up, he took a seat on the fireplace, took off his hat and wiped his brow. Kate was standing speechless in the corner. He told her to sit down on the bed so he could sort this out. She did so, but real nervous like."

"What happened next?" Agent Travis quietly asked.

Jack began to choke up and shook his head, looking away before he got up, apparently done talking for the moment. Agent Travis rose with him, studying his movements, making sure none of them were in the direction of his pistol. They weren't. It looked like he just needed to stretch his legs and regain his composure. Jack walked in a small circle, ending up back where he began.

Agent Travis waited patiently before sensing the time was right to try again. He asked, "Son, what's your full name?"

Jack put his thumbs in his belt and stared at the ground, seeming to be in no hurry to answer the question. Travis decided to wait him out this time. After nearly a full minute of silence Jack's head raised up. Agent Travis caught his gaze as the young man said, "My name is Jack Pepper, of Logan, Utah."

5

Jack watched while Agent Travis went to his car and pulled out a notepad. He placed it on the hood of the car and began writing. Jack stepped away to collect his thoughts about how it all came to this. It used to be so simple. Days filled with hunting rabbits, exploring caves, fishing at Tony Grove Lake; all in these beautiful canyons. It almost felt like another life.

Jack peeked over his shoulder to see Travis scribbling away furiously, the sun gleaming off the car's black paint, creating a sort of aura around him. With Travis fully devoted to his notebook for the moment, Jack turned away and thought about the girl who was driving his willingness to cooperate.

He recalled the day he first met Kate Austin. They were both twelve years old. The Pepper family farm was only a little ways from a development of new homes popping up on the east bench. Kate's father was the county judge and doing very well. Their family had built a large new home there for Kate and her four siblings. She was the baby of the family and the only girl, giving her a special place in her father's heart. He beamed about her every chance he could get. Beautiful, bright, energetic, refined; all words Jack had heard the Judge use when describing his daughter. She told Jack she had grown accustomed to the praise and generally ignored it, although she wouldn't infringe on his right to be a proud father. It didn't much matter to Jack either. He knew Kate well enough now to know she was set on being her own woman and not the stereotype her father had created for her.

It was overcast the Saturday morning they first met. Jack was headed up to Green Canyon when he spotted a group of rabbits popping in and out of their warren at a distance of about 50 yards. They were busy at play, and nibbling on grass, and didn't see him come over the hill. Always eager to hone his skills with a .22 he laid down slowly in a prone position. Out of his peripheral vision he spotted a large rock and reached for it, his eyes never leaving the target. After slowly placing the rock an arm's length in front of him, he placed the end of the barrel quietly on top of it and brought his head down next to it, carefully lining up the front sight.

He spent some time looking for the most difficult shot, not the easy target. He already knew he could make that shot, but he wanted to stretch himself, find a tough angle through a bush or hit a specific spot. He was always up for a challenge.

While he was in the midst of sizing up a gray bunny with long ears he heard a voice, coming from directly behind him, say, 'are you going to shoot that rabbit or just stare it?' Startled that someone had got the drop on him, he rose up on his arms and wheeled around to see who it was.

Standing in front of him was a girl, about his size, not even ten yards away. She had straight brown hair that ran past her shoulders and down her back, with chestnut brown eyes that were almost a perfect match to her hair. Her skin was fair with freckles clustering on each cheek, while her red lips united together without a hint of expression one way or another. He didn't know who she was. All he knew was he couldn't take his eyes off of her.

Apparently surprised by his lack of response, she started again, "Well it's too late," as she began to walk towards him, pointing her finger in the direction of the rabbits. "They're all gone now," she said.

Jack just lay there staring at her while she walked up to him. She came right up to within a foot of him and looked down. She looked like a giant from his view. Realizing that he had yet to say anything, he got up hastily, dusted himself off and peered out to where the bunnies had been a few moments ago. "Oh, that's ok," he stammered, trying to think of something to say. "I didn't need to shoot them."

"Then why were you aiming at 'em?" Kate said, with a wry look on her face that brought the corners of her mouth up into a smile.

"Just practicing, I guess," Jack replied.

"Are you a good shot?" Kate asked, genuinely interested.

Jack looked down at his feet, not one to talk himself up.

"Well, you would have had to been to make that shot."

This intrigued Jack. "Do you know how to shoot?" he asked.

She looked at him again briefly before saying, "let's find out," while reaching for his rifle. He didn't protest as she grabbed it. Instead he was staring down at where her hand had made contact with his. Within a few seconds she was firing rounds into the trunk of a tree just past where the rabbits had been eating, before handing the rifle back to Jack, as if that answered the question.

"Where are we going?" she asked next, as if that was the only logical question to ask.

Confused by the 'we' part, he shrugged his shoulders and started walking towards his original destination in the canyon, curious to see if she would follow.

Kate followed lock step. She must have recognized he was a bit shy as she took over the conversation, which suited Jack just fine. She started on about how she didn't know many kids on this side of town and how she was bored since school was out for the summer. She told him about her family, about her dad being the judge and her older brothers. She talked about how her mother was from the country and made sure she knew how to ride and how to shoot, in equal amounts of time to her piano and singing lessons. It was a good 15 minutes of Austin family history before she came up for air.

The break didn't last long. Jack focused on kicking rocks down the trail, dreading the question he knew was coming.

"How about your family?" she finally asked.

Jack didn't know what to say so he kept it short, in typical Jack fashion. He didn't want to tell her the real story as it paled in comparison to her family life. His father, Thomas, grew up in Northern Utah but spent time in Arizona working cattle in his early twenties. His mother, Alejandra (or Allie to her friends), was Hispanic but living in Arizona with her family. They met through friends and dated briefly before getting married, heading up to Utah afterwards to settle. They bought a small piece of land where they raised mostly cows and sheep, and grew what they could on the rest of it. It wasn't much of a life, but it taught Jack how to work, and he was happy being outdoors.

But those were the highlights. The fact is they struggled at times to make ends meet. Not to the point of receiving handouts, but it did require his father to work long hours. Those long hours over a period of long years wore his father down. He was not a loving father figure most of the time, more of a boss giving orders. He never showed much affection either, an occasional pat on the back or a 'good job' was as far as Tom went with his praise.

On bad days however, his temper would fly, followed by his fists. Never at Jack, only his mother. His father never treated her the same way Jack saw other men treat their wives. He wondered if it was because she had brown skin; that is, when it wasn't black and blue. Regardless, he didn't think highly of his father because of it. At some point, he just started calling him Tom. It was easier to disconnect his feelings that way. Jack didn't grow up angry, he just grew up, learning that emotions led to mistakes.

However, when he was free to roam the Cache countryside, like he was on that day, he was able to feel happy.

After a 45-minute hike, Kate asked again, "Where did you say we are going?"

"This is it," Jack replied as he led her off the trail and into a small plot of land deep inside the canyon. "It belongs to William Hendricks. It has a house, a stream and a cave. Probably more too but I am still checking it out. He told me I could look around up here as long as I don't disturb the cows."

"William Hendricks? I think we met their family. They came over when we moved in." she said, trying to recall the details. "Does he have a boy our age?"

"Yeah, that's Billy. He's in our class at school. I see him up here from time-to-time helping his dad."

"Do you know him very well?" Kate asked.

"A little I guess," Jack said, his voice trailing off. Kate didn't yet realize exactly how much of a loner Jack really was. As if the family finances weren't already a hindrance to acceptance, combining that with a small family of one child and brown skin in Utah, he might as well have been invisible, which explains why he usually kept to himself, and kept quiet.

"Come on, I'll show you around," Jack said.

They spent the afternoon exploring the stream and along the mountain.

Jack was amazed at how interested Kate was in the beauty of the land, like finding deer tracks or climbing a tree to see what's in a nest. The two couldn't have been more at home together. It didn't take long for a bond to start to grow.

Jack remembered the excitement he felt from having someone around that understood him. He opened up more that morning then he had with anyone else, actually talking and carrying on a conversation. It was a great feeling to finally have, he thought. He didn't recognize what it was then, but he did now. It was a purpose, a feeling of belonging. As time would pass and they got older, it would turn into something else. His world had changed that day for the better. And despite all the hardships he now faced, to him, it was all still worth it.

Jack blinked a couple of times as he came back to reality, realizing someone had said his name.

"Jack," Agent Travis said for the second time, reaching out from behind to grab his elbow. Jack spun around in a hurry, looking momentarily dazed.

"Whoa, easy," Travis said as he took a step back and put his hands up in a peaceful gesture. "What do you say we get back to it?" as he gestured towards the rocks. "I need to know what happened next in the cabin."

6

Agent Travis watched Jack closely as he made his way back to the rock to sit down. Travis worked to estimate his age. Jack had a youthful appearance, but it was overshadowed by the troubled glint in his brown eyes. His skin was light brown, smooth, lacking wrinkles, and his dark hair crested down over his forehead, hiding the worry that filled his brow. Travis noted his eyes were also a little blood-shot, like he had been lacking sleep. In all aspects, Jack's appearance seemed to be in contrast, being young and old all at once.

"How old are you, Jack?" Agent Travis asked.

"Twenty-one," Jack replied.

Travis studied him again before nodding his acceptance. "And where have you been staying?" he continued.

The question made Jack squirm. "Not far," he eventually replied.

Sensing he didn't have enough rapport built yet to delve far into personal issues, Agent Travis shifted back to the story, notepad now in hand. "Ok, so last you said you and Kate were being held hostage by this large man out in a cabin."

"Hideout," Jack corrected him. "It's where they were holed up."

"Who are they? You've only mentioned one man."

"Well, it didn't take long for Eddie to start talking," said Jack.

"Wait," Agent Travis interrupted. "You know his name? How?"

"Yeah, that's what his gang calls him, Fast Eddie." Jack said.

"You're sure?" Agent Travis continued, with a skeptical look. He couldn't believe Jack was actually in possession of the bank robber's identity.

"I'm sure," Jack said with a decisive assurance, as if he wished he didn't know.

"Ok," Agent Travis said, easing off so Jack could continue, "so what did he start talking about?"

"Well, he started by saying we were the luckiest couple of degenerates he ever met, because we somehow got past his lookouts and so close to their hideout. That we were lucky we weren't already dead. He asked a couple times if we were alone or if we were followed. Kate did most of the talking, or all of it really. She looked real worried. I can still see her face in my mind – that expression. It wasn't good." Jack said as he shook his head lightly. With a deep breath, he started again.

"Fast Eddie, you know, he talks a lot, more than a man should talk, especially given what he'd done," Jack said.

Agent Travis again wanted to pounce on that one but instead decided to let Jack go a little longer.

"So he starts telling us that he has guys staked out in the woods watching the road and the trails. We had come in the back way on a path Kate and I use sometimes. No one uses it but us. We rode two of her horses, Sunset and Bridget, from the northwest and over the ridge. We tied them up a little ways back and were on foot. They wouldn't have been looking for us back there. So he thinks we're lucky and all I think is he's ignorant because he's hiding in plain sight to me. He obviously doesn't know Logan very well."

"Even though Kate is telling him we weren't looking for him, he doesn't believe her. He starts asking what she knows and if she is here for the money. Kate says 'what money?' and he points to a couple large, black canvas bags sitting on the floor by the fireplace, his temper rising and falling along the way. Then he acts like he is going to hit her if she doesn't confess. She covered her face but he didn't hit her, at least not yet. I could see she was about to cry."

Jack was straining now for the words but continued, "As for me, I was getting angry. Angry that we were caught. Angry about how he was treating her. Angry that I got myself locked up. I kept trying to figure out how we were going to get out. I rattled the stove, trying to move it, but it didn't budge. That's when Eddie left her and came over to me and said 'you ain't going nowhere boy' and finished the sentence with his fist in my face. Broke my nose. It hurt something fierce. I crouched down and it started bleeding all over. He thought that was real funny. He has this laugh he likes to make. It sounds like he's wheezing for air and getting choked in the process, but that's how he laughs. I've heard it a few times now and I don't care to ever hear it again."

"So you've spent some time with this Fast Eddie?" Travis asked intuitively.

"More than I wanted to but not by choice," Jack said.

"What did Eddie do after he hit you?" Agent Travis asked.

"He went back to the fireplace and sat down, looked like he needed to rest. His face was red and he was sweating like the rain," said Jack. "After a few minutes, he starts talking again. Starts telling us how smart he is. How he fooled everyone with the great Cache County Bank robbery, at least that is how he put it. Kate shot me a look when she realized what exactly was in the bags. I held her gaze for a moment but then looked down. I was afraid she could see what I was thinking."

"What were you thinking?" said Travis.

Jack straightened up, fixed his eyes right on Agent Travis and said, "That we were dead."

Travis soaked in the information, before promptly coming to the same conclusion. If what Jack was saying is true, no doubt Fast Eddie meant to kill them, if he was divulging that kind of information. While processing what he was hearing, Jack started talking again.

"I think he just couldn't wait to brag about it. So he starts in on how there are these tunnels under the bank branch on Main street. They connect to the building next to it, go out to the street for unloading coal for the boiler, and under the parking lot. Part of the tunnels belong to the bank and the other part for the sewer. Well apparently Eddie has a guy with him that worked on the pipes for the sewer and he has seen the metal door that blocks the way into the basement of the bank. Because the pipe he is fixing runs into bank property, he had the key for a whole day while he worked on it. And what does he do? He hurries over on a lunch break to another one of Eddie's guys who makes a copy. By the end of the day, the pipe is fixed but the bank is busted. At least that is what he said. He got a good laugh out of that."

Travis knew exactly the door Jack was talking about, the tunnels too. He had always felt they could be somehow connected to the robbery. Not only were they unusual but he had deemed them a vulnerability. If anyone knew the way down into the sewer and to that metal door, they would have complete cover underground to get in and out. That meant that the broken window at street level was a diversion, something Agent Travis felt was out of place.

But knowing about the tunnels wouldn't have been enough, he thought. It would have required access to the basement door. A thorough inspection of the door and lock hadn't revealed any unusual fingerprints or other clues. The only way in would have been with a key. So far the story Jack was telling held true.

"Did he mention their names?" Travis finally said to Jack.

"I know their names," Jack said. "Donovan, Jimmy, Will and Duke. That last one, Duke. He's the one that worked on the sewer."

"So you've seen these men?"

"Yes," Jack replied. "I've seen them."

"Were they there that day?" Agent Travis asked as his voice filled with purpose.

"I assume they were there but I didn't see them then. Not on that day," Jack continued. "They were out watching the road and trails I guess. That is why Eddie was so surprised we got through without them seeing us."

Travis wrote down the names, but feeling like he was beginning to be taken in by Jack and his story, he wanted to circle back to see if he could rattle Jack, make him contradict himself, just to be sure he wasn't being played for a fool.

"Jack," Agent Travis said as he stood and walked to a spot where Jack had to look up into the sun, "I want to get this straight. You're telling me that an armed gang of four or five dangerous men, who had just pulled off a risky bank robbery, were hiding in the woods outside Logan and you somehow stumbled upon them on a nature walk, and they, or he, immediately confessed to the crime, telling you the whole story. Is that right?"

Jack looked down at his boots for a long minute before he raised his head, squinting into the sun, and gave a resounding, "Yep."

"You can understand though how I might be slow to believe a story like this," Travis said, pausing for effect, "from a man who sent me a secret message to meet him alone in the woods."

Jack replied directly, "I never said to come alone."

Agent Travis readjusted after that misstep, "Still, you brought me all the way up here to give me some 'information' and now you are telling me well, basically every detail, as if you had been at the bank yourself," Agent Travis said, his voice driving higher. "Doesn't that seem a little implausible?"

Travis watched Jack closely for a response, but Jack just sat there, sitting in the sun, clearly not about to speak. Travis held his ground too, awaiting a response. He knew that you could learn as much from a suspect from what they don't say as what they do say and he was waiting for Jack to give up any kind of clues. But Jack just sat there, void of expression, content to let the time pass.

Finding Jack unwilling to deviate from his story, Agent Travis eased off and said, "Ok, how about we assume you are telling the truth? That would explain how they got into the bank but it doesn't explain how they knew that a large sum of money was coming into town that day. Anything you want to tell me about that?"

"They didn't know, at least that is what Eddie said. He started talking about how they were planning to go in late Saturday night but while he was staking out the place he saw the courier pull up and started unloading bags, large black bags that looked like they were full, and heavy. So he says he brought the gang together that night to do the place. They went in just after midnight, cleaned the place out in less than four hours. Four hours for three hundred thousand. At least that is what he said, and he was plenty proud when he said it. Fast Eddie thinks a lot about his bank robbing skills."

Befuddled by what he was hearing, Agent Travis sat back down. He took out a handkerchief and wiped off a bead of sweat. Could it have been that simple, he thought? A maintenance worker gains access through a basement door in an unknown tunnel, combined with dumb luck on the timing of the cash shipment? Whether he was ready to fully believe it or not, the story did fit. From what he had already learned this morning from Jack, it would change everything in this case.

His adrenaline was flowing freely now, but there was one more obvious question that needed to be asked. One question that threw the whole story into doubt. One question that if Jack couldn't answer definitively, would require Agent Travis to hold this young man as the top suspect.

"Jack, I hate to tell you this, but that doesn't explain why you're still alive."

7

Jack thought about that. It's true, he should be dead, probably a few times. The hideout was not meant for them to survive. He also should have been killed later in St. George. And even before that when his mom finally left.

Although it was a shock, he never blamed her for going. He understood. Living in a small town like Logan, in an almost entirely white population, without any of her family around, a husband prone to violent outbursts and, for whatever reason, only being able to bear one child; these were all burdens she had carried for a long time. None of them matched a typical northern Utah life. In the end, Tom's fists proved stronger than her will to resist. Despite being seemingly patient with her trials, late one evening, just after dusk, she slipped out quietly, never to return.

It left Jack feeling abandoned and even more reticent than before, especially given she hadn't mentioned a word of it before leaving, not even to say goodbye. That was the hardest part.

A few days after, someone said they saw her with a group of migrant workers headed north in Idaho. Jack immediately wanted to go find her but Tom wouldn't let him. He said she had made her choice. Their home was in Logan and there would be no chasing after her. He could tell Tom was now the one hurting, from his hands thrown in anger. Besides, Jack knew Tom wouldn't have known how to make it right even if they did find her. He concluded that more than anything likely kept Tom from looking.

Jack was fifteen at the time. He had contemplated leaving too but where would he go? This is the only place he had ever known. During one particularly low night, he and Trigger went out alone to look at the stars. That night, while lying on the soft grass in a neighbor's field, looking up to heaven, he wondered if he shouldn't pull out his revolver and make quick work of himself. After some silent deliberation and counting up what he had to live for, he calculated the answer was decidedly yes.

On his last birthday Tom had given him a revolver as a gift. It was an older gun but it was his first pistol so he didn't mind that it was used. He had bought a holster and took the gun with him any time he went out exploring, and he had it with him that night. Following his mom's example of leaving without so much as a goodbye, he got up, stood up straight, and pulled out his gun. The night air was cool. He felt a warm breeze blow across his face, creating a peaceful sort of feeling as he put the cold steel of the gun to his head and cocked the hammer, ready to accept his self-imposed fate.

But before he could fire, Trigger did something he rarely does. He began barking incessantly, as if he was warding off an unseen intruder. It was unusual to hear him bark at all, especially so wildly, and Jack noted a strange pitch to the sound. It was enough that Jack momentarily forgot about his suicide plan. Instead, he started asking Trigger what was the matter? Before long, his seemingly possessed dog ran off into the brush and disappeared. Jack went running after him. After a lengthy run, with Jack going through every conceivable possibility on what set Trigger off, he finally caught up to him. Trigger had stopped running, and stopped barking. In fact, he was standing completely silent, except for the panting, looking up at Jack.

"What is it?" Jack demanded while leaning over, hands on knees, annoyed that he had just been forced to give his best Jesse Owens impression. Trigger turned and looked behind him. As Jack straightened up to look, he realized their path had taken them directly to Kate's house, which was now just a short distance away, and directly in Trigger's line of sight.

Confused by what was happening, Jack looked down at his dog again, who was now staring back up at him, as if to say 'there is still one thing worth living for.' Jack looked from Trigger to Kate's house and back again, before turning his gaze back to the sky above, wondering what it all meant.

Jack had not been raised to be religious, despite being surrounded by Latter-day Saints his whole life. Their family had been invited to church several times by their neighbors, Kate's family included, but religion wasn't high on Tom's priority list so they rarely went. That left him ill-equipped to interpret his current situation. What he did know is he no longer wanted to end his life.

Instead, he decided maybe he had discounted his feelings for Kate when calculating what he had to live for. Deep down there was a strong desire to always be with her. If he hadn't already fallen in love with her, he did that night while staring at her house from a distance, with millions of stars witnessing from above. She would never know the part she played in beginning to heal the wound left by his mother's departure but on that night she had saved his life; with help, of course, from his other best friend, Trigger. And he now felt it was his duty, and privilege, to watch over both of them.

The weight of Agent Travis' stare brought Jack back to the present. He was standing, waiting patiently. It wasn't a question that was going to pass without an answer, Jack knew that.

"You're right, I haven't explained that. I should be dead. That might have made things easier," he trailed off. "But that would have involved me doing nothing while I watched Eddie attack her. That was not something I could let happen."

Agent Travis shifted his feet and said almost apologetically, with an obvious concern in his voice, "Eddie attacked Kate?"

"I guess he had grown tired with us, and realized it was time to make sure we never repeated his story. He walked over to the window and looked around to make sure no one was coming. Then he walked towards me and grabbed at the handcuffs, checking to make sure it was connected tightly to the stove, while he looked me right in the eye, and made this ugly sort of grin before he steps away. Then he turns towards Kate and says in his disgusting voice, 'Doll, you look like you're about ready for a real man,' as he slid his hand down his fat stomach, resting his hand on his belt. 'Well, you're in luck. I think I might just help you out with that,' he says."

Travis sat slowly back down on the rock while Jack continued, speaking even softer now, as he relived it again in his mind. "Kate had a look of terror in her eyes. She was unable to move from where she sat on the bed. The blood had drained from her face and her gaze was locked on to Eddie's movements. He took another step towards her. I needed her to snap out of it. I yelled, Run!" Jack said in a loud voice as if re-enacting it for Agent Travis.

"What did she do?" Travis asked, hanging on Jack's every word.

"She broke free from her trance, looked at me for a split second, before getting up and bolting for the door," Jack said. "I thought she might make it but it turns out Eddie is fast for his size. He lunged at her and caught a hand full of her hair as she went by. It took her clean off her feet and she landed hard on her back with a pain-filled scream. Eddie says `yeah, I'll make you scream, that's for sure' and he starts dragging her across the floor boards by her hair, back to the bed. She's kicking and fighting now but he keeps his grip and stays behind her, so to be out of her reach."

"When he has her back at the bed, he reaches down, grabs her by the throat and picks her up. I can hear her choking now. Eddie slams her on the bed and puts a knee down on her, right under the ribs. She's still struggling, which I think he likes because now he's just taunting her, loosening his grip on her throat to let her gasp for air and then tightening it again, all the while saying stuff like 'I am gonna show you what you were made for' or something like that."

"Still she kept fighting the best she could, even got him across the face with her nails. It made Eddie step back and release his grip. She quickly crawled backwards on the bed to the wall, as far from him as she could, but she's still cornered. He stops to check his face for blood, calls her some more nasty names, before lunging forward to grab her by the ankle. Now that he has a hold of her again, he pulls her forward with one quick swipe," Jack continued while demonstrating so Agent Travis could see, "and leans in with his full weight to land a hard right across her face."

Jack paused, checking his emotions, before he continued, "I've seen a man hit a woman. I know what it looks like, what it sounds like, but I've never seen that before. He hit her like she was a man, no mercy, gave it all he's got. She didn't fight anymore after that. She didn't speak. She didn't do nothing. I saw her eyes blinking so I know she isn't entirely out but I actually wished to God that she was, so she didn't have to be awake for what was coming."

Jack paused again. "He knows he has her now so he reaches down and grabs her by the legs, sliding her to him, with her legs dangling off the bed, one on either side of him. I yelled, Stop! Eddie paused to look back with that same ugly smile and says `boy, I'm gonna teach you something…white women belong to white men, not some nothing field rat like you. You just sit there and think about that while I enjoy my spoils.' That's all he says before turning back to Kate. Then he straightens up and starts taking off his holster and belt. I am pulling at the handcuffs and the stove but I can't get free."

Agent Travis interrupted, "There is nothing you could have done, Jack. It's not your fault." A moment of silence passed between them while Jack moved the dirt around on the ground with his boot.

"Actually, there was one thing I could do," Jack replied as he glanced up with that determined look returning to his eyes. "Because, you see, my gun is where Fast Eddie had left it on the table, maybe six feet out of my reach, and Eddie had his back to me now. I looked down at my right hand and decided I've got to pull it through. So I drop to the floor and put my feet on the stove and pull as hard as I can on my right arm. It hurt like the dickens but, sure enough, I hear my thumb break with a pop. Despite the pain, I don't make a sound and Eddie doesn't bother to look back. I guess he figures I am struggling in vain. Well, he doesn't even have his pants down yet when I get to my gun. Holding it in my left hand, I draw up on him and cock the trigger."

"This he definitely hears `cause he freezes. I don't even have to tell him to turn around. He starts around slowly, hands at his side, with his gun belt lying on the opposite bunk. I expected he would be scared but the look of anger in his eye told me this man has been in tough spots before and he must have lived through it so I don't want to take any chances. I am already holding the gun in the wrong hand and he's no more than 10 feet from me. The cabin went silent and I have him locked in my sights. I don't know exactly how long the silence lasted but eventually he goes to speak and I fire one off."

"I see a spurt of blood come out of his neck as he recoils. But he doesn't go down. Instead, he lunges towards me as I shift right and fire off two more rounds. His momentum carries him forward and he comes to a rest face down on the fireplace, straddling the bags of money. I keep my gun on him, waiting for movement, but he just laid there, dead where he fell."

Jack looked up to see a look of astonishment on Agent Travis' face, his mouth parted yet speechless. He let it sink in for the Agent, who, for the first time all morning, didn't have the upper hand.

Realizing he was struggling to form his next question, Jack continued, "When the shots rang out it must have brought Kate back because I hear her softly call my name. I went over to help her. I leaned down and she reached up with both hands and grabbed my hands. I winced and pulled back my right hand. She looked at it and asked what was wrong. I said nothing, just helped her to her feet so we could get out of there. She was woozy for those first few steps. I had to practically carry her until she got her legs back. But she came around and we were quick to put some distance between us and the hideout, heading out the way we came in so not to cross paths with anyone else from his gang."

"We made it back to the horses. I helped Kate onto Bridget and I was about to mount Sunset when I hear a rustling behind me. I wheel around, gun drawn again, but there was no one around. Instead, out from behind a scrub oak walks Trigger, badly limping, but alive. I darn near couldn't believe it. He had made his way back and sat to wait for us. I remember thinking he must be the toughest dog in all of Utah. I picked him up and carried him in the saddle with me. He never whimpered once the entire way home."

"Wait a minute," Agent Travis said, cutting back into the conversation now, "if you left Eddie there, with the money, what do you think happened to him, and the money?" asking what was a fairly obvious question to Jack.

"His gang must've come back and seen what happened," Jack replied indifferently.

Discouraged, Agent Travis said, "That's it then?"

Realizing Agent Travis wanted more, Jack perked up and said, "Well, I wasn't about to hang around and ask."

He watched Agent Travis get up and walk back towards his car, rubbing his face in the process. Sensing Agent Travis' disappointment, Jack decided to lift his spirits and said, "Agent Travis, there's more to the story."

8

Agent Travis turned around and sized up Jack who was still sitting. He looked at his watch, nearly 11 am. Their conversation had already burned up a good portion of the morning and he still didn't have that one piece of definitive information that would lead to an arrest and recovery of the money. Jack had quite a story and some of the facts matched the evidence, but now hearing the mastermind and the money have vanished, and Jack has limited information on the other gang members, this still wouldn't do. If there was more to the story it would have to contain hard evidence in order to be of any value.

Travis felt a grumbling in his stomach. His early morning departure combined with the added excitement of working a case in the field left him hungry. He went around to the passenger side of his car, opened the door and leaned in. He reemerged with a brown paper bag. It was the lunch Sarah had made for him. He pulled out a meat-and-cheese sandwich cut into two parts.

As he removed the wrapper, he walked back over to Jack and, with no words, offered him half. Jack hesitated at first but Travis held it out closer as a sign he insisted. This time Jack reached up to accept the offering, also with no words, except for an easy nod meant as a thank you.

"Jack," Travis said after swallowing a few bites, "I've got to be honest. I was hoping to have something more substantial, possibly some physical evidence I could use to corroborate your story. You're leaving me in a tough spot here. I might have to ask you to come back with me with to Salt Lake while we sort this all out."

Chewing slowly and taking his time formulating an answer, Jack responded, "I can't do that. Kate is in danger. I can't leave her."

"How do you know Kate is danger?" Agent Travis said as he leaned back against his car putting one foot on the bumper in a relaxed manner.

"As I said, there is more to the story," Jack answered as he squinted to look up at Agent Travis, a hint of desperation in his eye.

"There better be a lot more or we may need to be leaving soon," Agent Travis said, trying to instill the importance of full cooperation on the young man. He now knew he could use a trip to Salt Lake as leverage to get the facts that were slow in coming.

He watched closely as Jack finished his sandwich, wiping his hands on his jeans, before starting back into the story. "Well as I said, we rode home. We went back to stable her horses. While we were doing that we talked, knowing that there were going to be a lot of questions about my thumb and her face and neck. Given the history of abuse with Tom and my mother, we knew it might not look so good."

"Why not just tell the truth?" Agent Travis asked with a questioning look.

"What truth? Our truth…that we were attacked by bank robbers hiding in the woods? It's only the truth if people believe you, Agent Travis," Jack said with a pained expression. "Exactly how was that going to look, when they go to investigate and find nothing? Odds are the gang, the body, the money were all long gone. We knew that. If so, it would lead back to a girl with a head injury and a boy from a broken home with a busted hand. No, that wouldn't do. Not with her father being the county judge. Even if I wasn't arrested, you could be rest assured he would make it so we never saw each other again. No, sometimes the truth comes up short to another man's reasons. What about you Agent Travis? Are you willing to hear the truth or are you looking for your own reasons?"

Agent Travis breathed long with an undecided look. That was a big thought from such a young man, but one who obviously had plenty of time to mull it over in the past two years. He could see the dilemma but didn't want to encourage this choice of dishonesty. He generally believed it was best to be forthcoming in all situations, letting the consequences fall where they may.

Travis spoke next, deliberately avoiding Jack's question in order to maintain control of the conversation without wasting time on tangents, "So how did that work out for you?"

"There are a lot of things that could have been different, but they weren't. I don't dwell on it. I am here now because I am trying to set things right," said Jack.

"No, you're here now because you are at a dead end and you need my help. You can have it but it comes with expectations, Jack. The help I'm offering is conditional. I want the full truth."

Agent Travis watched as Jack looked at the dirt. He didn't seem afraid or annoyed; he just seemed to be waiting. Travis rolled his eyes before pushing off his car and heading back to the rock to continue. "Ok Jack, so then what? Your hand got better I see."

Jack looked down and wiggled his fingers and thumb back and forth.

"It did," Jack said, "I had to see the doctor but he checked it out to make sure it set right. When he asked me what happened I told him it caught when a rock shifted on to it while exploring a cave and I had to pull it free. Kate came up with a similar story, saying that she slipped and fell while running to help me in the dim light of the cave. It wasn't great but it got us by, just barely. Her father never cared much for me to begin with but now I had no chance with him. He must have told Kate to stop spending time with me because I didn't see her much after that, and when I did she seemed to be holding back."

"But a few weeks went by, and then a few months, we had all healed up. Trigger too. I thought life might just return to normal. Normal wasn't great to begin with but after what we went through, I was alright with normal for a while. Unfortunately it turns out I was wrong," Jack said.

"What do you mean?"

"Well it started one night, late. I had already turned in for the night. Tom must have still been up because I can see the light coming in under my door. Trigger was in the room with me, sleeping on the end of the bed as he usually does. We must have both heard it together because his head came up the same time as mine."

"What did you hear?" Agent Travis said curiously.

"Footsteps, just outside the house. There was no mistaking it. It was the steps of a man walking at a slow pace. I wondered if Tom had heard them too but he had been drinking so I assumed not. Or if he did, he didn't say anything. I listened to them move here and there for a few minutes, trying to decide if it warranted a closer look or if I was just being paranoid. There could have been a simple explanation," Jack said.

"So you didn't investigate?" Agent Travis asked.

"Not that time. But they came back again the next night. I looked out the window that time but didn't see anything. I thought about going out to have a look around but something told me that wouldn't be a good idea so I didn't. Just laid there until they went away and then tried to sleep. But it was tough. My mind was spinning."

Jack moved some dirt around with his boot again. Travis decided that was a tell he must have when he is nervous. He was content to let him push that dirt around all day for a good piece of information.

Jack continued, "It wasn't until the next day that I knew something was seriously wrong. Tom and I had driven into town for some supplies. We had a few stops to make and were gone most of the morning. When we came back we found our place ransacked. Someone had been there and gone through everything. A little bit of money was taken, along with a silver pocket watch that belonged to Tom, handed down from his father, but mostly stuff was just thrown around like they were looking for something."

"Who did you suspect?" Agent Travis said.

"Well Tom started guessing names from around town, mostly some of the younger guys I had known in school but I had a feeling it was connected to that day in the canyon. We didn't have enemies around town and if we did they would have known we had very little to steal. I didn't sleep much after that day. And when I did, I kept my gun loaded on the nightstand next to me. But it wasn't so much me that I was worried about. It was Kate," Jack said.

"Did you tell her about what was happening at your house?" said Travis.

"I did," Jack replied in a serious tone. "We would still see each other on occasion but only when Kate could come up with an excuse to get away. Fortunately, we saw each other that next day and I told her. I asked her if she had seen anything suspicious around her house but she said no. It was then I realized how handy it was to have a judge for a father. It made me feel better too. It was much less likely anything would happen to her as long as she was living at home. So we agreed to keep to our routines and I would start doing some investigating of my own to sort it out."

"The next night Trigger and I struck out at dusk and headed up the canyon. I went back to their hideout to see what was doing there. Sure enough, as I approached, staying low in the brush, there was light from the fireplace flickering from the window. That sight put a knot right in my stomach. I knew it was bad. The only ones to use that cabin in the past ten years, other than me, was the gang that robbed the bank," Jack said.

Agent Travis was encouraged by the turn of events and broke in on Jack to ask, "Did you see anyone through the window?"

"I saw a couple men walk by on occasion. One came out to relieve himself too but I didn't recognize either of them," Jack answered.

"What did they look like?" Agent Travis continued.

"The one from the window looked normal enough. He was a white guy, normal size, nothing out of the ordinary but the other guy, who stepped outside, he was much larger. Must have been at least six foot, five inches tall, well-built and had blonde hair. It was hard to see with the limited light but he was clearly someone you wouldn't want to mess with," Jack said, appearing to think carefully about the description.

"I kept an eye on them from a distance all night but they never left the cabin. I eventually went home once the light from the fire inside the hideout went out, got in just before 4 am. When it came time to get to work the next day I was too tired. Lack of sleep from the past couple nights had caught up to me. I told Tom I was sick and couldn't work. He didn't question it because I was never one to shuck my work."

At that Jack stopped abruptly, rose to his feet, walking a few steps away, before putting his hands on his hips.

Travis had been watching and learning Jack's patterns and he knew this meant Jack had reached a point in the story that was difficult for him. Agent Travis waited patiently, jotting down a few things in his notepad while the seconds ticked away.

When Jack did speak again, he did so with his back to Agent Travis and head hung slightly. His comments stopped Travis' writing cold.

"That was the last time I saw Tom alive."

9

Jack waited for a minute to give Agent Travis time to digest it. It had been a year and he hadn't fully come to grips with it himself. He didn't approve of the choices Tom had made and what it had done to their family but he knew Tom wasn't without his own merits. He presumed the root of much of his anger was based on the fact that his life hadn't turned out as he had hoped. Yet, he still got up each morning and tried to provide for them. It may not have made up for all the wrongs he had caused with his drinking and violence but Jack could respect his work ethic.

Tom was also the source of many of his outdoor skills. He wouldn't know how to raise crops or livestock if it wasn't for his father. He wouldn't know how to ride a horse or shoot a gun. He wouldn't know how to track deer. He wouldn't know how to survive. Even if Tom was the reason he now needed these skills, at least he didn't leave him empty-handed, he thought.

"You want to run that by me again?" Travis said, as his notepad tilted down towards the ground, along with his expression.

Jack walked back and eased back on to his rock. "My father is dead and it is because of me," Jack said, his face contorting in an unusual expression like the memory carried with it a physical pain. "I woke up sometime after noon that day and decided I better get out there to help with the work. The problem is I didn't know where Tom was. I looked around for a bit before I decided it would be easier by horseback. I saddled up and started riding to the other end of our land thinking he may be out working on a fence."

"As I come up over the hill on the east side I see him in the irrigation pond. I'm thinking to myself 'what's he doing in the water'. It made no sense. As I got closer, I can see he is lying face down, not moving. I jumped off my horse and ran over to him. The pond couldn't have been more than two feet deep that time of year. I waded in and got a hold of his jacket, pulling him to me. I could tell it was too late but I held on to him and kept calling his name. I don't know what I was expecting, a miracle maybe. It never came."

"What do you think happened, Jack?" Travis asked.

"I was in shock so I couldn't sort it out. Not yet anyway. I sat there for a bit but soon reckoned that I needed to get help. So I left him lying in the grass, raced back to the house and drove in to town to the police station," Jack said, depressed. He had thought about this many times but saying it out loud was harder than he thought.

He continued, "They came up to see him and went about their work. They sent me home to wait. After a while they came up to the house and told me he had a bad gash in his head. Their best guess was he slipped in mud and hit his head on a rock, causing him to pass out and drown. I was mad as could be because I know that's not the right answer but I am still stuck. If I start in with the whole story I would now be putting Kate in a tough spot and there would be no evidence of any of it. It would sound made up. So then I am just a kid with a dead father and a long story. How would that look to the police? I was the last person to see him alive and I am telling tales. No, I'm back in handcuffs if I say a word."

"Jack, I see the dilemma but that's how these things work. This dodging the truth can get out of control. It's hard to stop once set in motion. It's hard to go back," Agent Travis said empathetically, trying his best not to rub salt in a wound that was clearly still fresh in the young man's mind.

"I know that now. There's nothing I want more than to go back and do things different, but since that wasn't an option, I had no choice but to go forward," Jack replied.

"Ok, so then what? You think the gang killed your father? But how would they even know about you? You said they never saw you." Agent Travis continued.

"I know. It had me all mixed up. I wondered if they had heard the gunshots that day at their hideout, come running back and saw us leave. It doesn't account for the nearly ten months of peace we had afterwards but it's all I could figure at the time. And at the moment, I didn't really care how they put it together. I just knew I had to get out of here or Kate or I would be next," Jack said.

"So you told Kate what you were thinking? What did she say?" Agent Travis said.

"I did. I took Trigger and we went to see her that night. I knew I still wasn't welcome so I waited until I saw the light go on in her window and then I snuck up and knocked gently. She came over and pulled up the shade," Jack said with a smile forming on his face. "She was a sight for sore eyes. I swear she got prettier every day I knew I her, and on that night, it made me hurt inside to see her."

Jack glanced over to see if he was about to get one of Agent Travis' patented questions, knowing he might have shared too much, but he sat expressionless on the rock, waiting for Jack to continue. Jack took a double-take before concluding that Agent Travis wasn't the kind of guy you bluff in a game of cards.

"I could see on her face that she already knew about my father," Jack said next. "It's a small town. When someone dies, word gets around. She told me to go out to the horse stable and she would be out in a few minutes. I waited out there in the dark and she showed up shortly after, the moonlight giving her away as she opened the door. She quietly called my name and I stepped out so she could see me. I started to talk as she walked up to me but she didn't stop walking, just crashed into me and wrapped me up. She started to cry. It would be a few minutes before we started to talk. We just held on to each other."

"Eventually I pulled away and we started discussing what had happened. She agreed something seemed suspicious. Tom wouldn't have slipped and there was hardly a rock on the ground to hit. It was all too difficult to believe, especially after the footsteps and the break-in. She told me there had been no signs of trouble at her house. I was relieved to hear that. I am convinced now that her father's status kept the gang away from her."

"That does add up," Travis interjected.

"I told her I had a plan to solve the problem, knowing full well she wasn't going to like it," said Jack.

"I'm guessing I won't be thrilled with it either," Agent Travis said with a worried look. "What was your plan?"

"My plan was to lead them out of town. Clearly I was the one they were after. If I could draw them off, not having to worry about keeping her safe, then maybe I could resolve this one way or another. I had some business to take care of with burying my father but in a couple days' time I could be off, if I lived that long. I would make it real obvious too so they would be sure to follow," said Jack.

"What did Kate say about that?" Agent Travis said, reserving judgment on this new twist until he could hear more.

"She didn't care for it at first but she knew I was right. She asked how long I would be gone. I told her it could be a couple weeks, maybe more. She looked worried. I remember she asked me again later if I was coming back. I told her I was."

"We talked for a long time that night, about everything. I asked her if she would look after Trigger since I couldn't take him with me. She said yes. That seemed to make her feel better. She leaned down and scratched behind his ears and told him they were going to have so much fun. I was actually jealous of my dog there for a minute," Jack said with a half-hearted laugh. "When it was time for me to go, she stood up, got real close and gave me a kiss she knew I wouldn't soon forget. It worked. I haven't forgotten. Sometimes it's the only thing I choose to remember," Jack said, now staring contently ahead, unembarrassed.

"So you and Kate are boyfriend and girlfriend?" Agent Travis said presumptively.

Jack noted Travis was trying his best to not to make it uncomfortable, but he figured the question was eventually coming. He was prepared to answer. "Yes...at least I thought so," Jack replied.

"Do you want to elaborate on that?" Agent Travis asked while scribbling at his notebook again.

Why would I want to elaborate on that? Jack thought to himself before turning to Agent Travis with a straight-faced "No." He wasn't the only one who could hold his own in a game of poker.

"Ok, ok," Agent Travis said with a half-smile, "we'll come back to that one. Was that the last time you talked to her?"

"Yes," Jack said, as he reached up in an attempt to rub some of the anguish off his face. "We said our goodbyes and that was it. The next morning I started on my plan. I made arrangements for a quick burial for my father in the Logan Cemetery. I put our land and home up for sale and the lawyer I contacted, he fronted me some money to pay for the plot and headstone. He gave me some extra cash too for my trip. We had set it up that after the property sold, he would take his fees, including what he had loaned to me, and put the rest in an escrow account at the bank. That was it. Within a couple days it was time for the funeral and I was packed up to head out of town as soon as it ended."

"It surprises me you had even that much time. If what you are saying is true, I would think the gang would have come for you immediately, especially now that you were alone," Travis said.

"I thought the same thing but I guess in hindsight I was getting a lot of attention from the police and the neighbors following Tom's death. Even though I had already turned twenty, they treated me like an orphan and wanted to know that I was being cared for. That's the thing about Logan, people watch out for each other. It's always been that way up here. I think in this case all their attention probably protected me more than they know."

"So we held the funeral in the morning. It was a short service at the Latter-day Saint church by our house. Like I said, we weren't LDS, but they take care of you regardless. There were maybe 15-20 people who came to that. The Bishop was busy saying a few words and that's when I saw him," Jack said, halting now for effect.

Quickly jumping at the queue, "Saw who?" asked Agent Travis.

"Donovan," Jack said.

"Who's Donovan?" Travis countered.

"Remember the big guy I saw at their hideout that night. That's Donovan," Jack said.

Sensing Agent Travis was wondering how he knew his name, he continued. "It'll make sense in a minute. He is Fast Eddie's right hand man. A big guy, with an accent, I noticed him from his size and his blonde hair, which comes down his to neck. I don't know where he came from but he would stand out anywhere. Anyway, Logan cemetery is a big place and I see him off in the distance leaning against one of the trees, watching us.

He didn't do anything but watch and by the time the graveside service was over, he was gone. That's when I knew my time was up here in Logan."

"So as soon as I am done shaking hands, I went back to the house, picked up my bags and started walking towards town, headed to the train station at the end of Center Street. With each step, I thought it might be my last. I kept expecting him to pull up next to me and drag me off, but he never came. When I got there I bought a ticket and waited to board. I was conflicted then, at that moment. I wanted to get away but only if they followed. Otherwise, this wouldn't work."

"After what felt like forever the whistle blew and the conductor yelled 'all aboard.' I went aboard the train and took a seat, peering out the window the whole time. I didn't see Donovan anywhere on the platform. Soon the whistle blew again and we started to roll away. I was debating jumping off and going to find him, just to get it over with, but as we pulled out of the station, sure enough, there was Donovan leaning against the side of the building. He locked eyes on me, his gaze following me until we were out of sight. I knew then my planned had worked," Jack said, coming up for air.

"Where did you go?" Agent Travis asked.

"About as far away as I could think to go and still be close enough to get back if needed," Jack answered.

"And where was that?" said Travis.

"St. George. A long train ride but still in Utah," Jack said.

"Did it work? The getting away part," Agent Travis asked.

"It did. I was gone. It was the furthest away from home I had ever been. Went from the cool mountains to the heat of the desert, which was a whole new experience to me. It felt good to get away, like a vacation of sorts. I had left the past and my troubles behind," Jack said before pausing, "and just as expected, they followed me down south."

10

It was past 1 pm now. The late summer heat was bearing down. Agent Travis could feel his hands and neck beginning to burn, the sun wearing him down mentally as well. He looked around and spotted what looked like a good spot of shade under some Aspen trees. He turned to Jack with a "come on" while motioning for him to follow.

Once under the cover of the branches, Travis began to feel better. The temperature felt a good ten degrees cooler and the shade had a soothing effect on both his mind and body. It had been a long interview. He no longer felt like Jack was a threat but he also had yet to make up his mind on any of this. As much as he would have liked to be done and headed home, he needed to continue to dig. He was anxious to report to his boss about what he was hearing, but not until he had real evidence.

"Jack, what did you do once you got to St. George?" he asked as they settled down on the soft ground.

"Not much at first. I found a place to lodge and then started looking for work. After a couple of days I came across a man at the feed store that agreed to hire me on for some temporary work. It wasn't much, pushing cattle around is all, but it helped pass the time and allowed me to be outdoors," Jack said while twisting a blade of grass in his fingers. "I worried about Kate too but there wasn't much I could do about that at the moment. I knew she was safer with me gone so I just sort of settled into desert living," Jack said.

"How long was it until Donovan found you?" Agent Travis asked.

"Oh, not long, about three weeks I guess," Jack said. "I was finishing up dinner one night at this eatery I like. It's kind of a lonely thing to eat alone at every meal so I started staying late, just watching the families come and go. The staff was friendly to me. It kind of became my new home."

"So anyway, I was walking out of there, late one night, and I come around a corner and down the alley when I ran smack into Donovan's chest. It startles me and before I know it he's grabbed me and shoved me up against a wall. I can see that there are a few other men with him but my eyes didn't leave his. I am no longer carrying a gun as to not attract attention in the city so I am at his mercy," Jack said, discarding his blade of grass with a dejected look.

"But as fate has it, Donovan isn't the one calling the shots after all. Instead, I hear that fat man's voice come wheezing out from behind Donovan. He says 'let me see him.' Donovan slowly stepped aside with a devious smile, and now I am face-to-face with Fast Eddie. The man I shot and left for dead, resurrected before me."

"Instantly, it all makes sense. How they knew about me, why they were looking for me. I was half-relieved to know the truth, or at least I would have been if the other half wasn't so concerned about what's about to happen."

"What happened, Jack?" Travis asked, watching him closely.

Jack let out a sigh and said, "Eddie looks me up and down. I can see the scar from the bullet I put through his neck. He seems to have trouble breathing and I am guessing that was my doing. Then he gets real close, to the point where I can smell his stinking odor again. His face was inches from mine when he says 'nowhere left to run, boy. It's your day of reckoning.' And with that he hits me right up under the ribs. I am hunched over, coughing, and he starts saying how he was laid up for months in a hospital because of me. Couldn't talk. Could barely eat. Couldn't do much of anything except think about me and what he was going to do when he caught me."

Travis watched as Jack paused, his hand searching through the grass for just the right blade to pull next. After a few seconds, he lost interest and turned his attention back to Agent Travis and said, "I won't bore you with the grisly details but they worked me over pretty good. Then Eddie says, wheezing harder now, 'haul him to the back, put him in the trunk.' So they drag me down the alley and I am wondering if this is the end when all of sudden they stop dead in their tracks."

Travis stopped writing, hanging on Jack's next words.

"I look up to see a police car parked under a street lamp not twenty yards from us as we come out of the alley. I couldn't believe my luck. I realize this is my chance and I pull free and start walking away down the street. The police car pulls forward slowly to get a better look at Eddie and the boys, which makes them turn immediately back down the alley in the opposite direction. I can hear Eddie cursing as he goes. I figure I am about the luckiest person on earth at that moment."

"Jack, how many men were with him?" Agent Travis asked as he readied his notebook again.

"It was Eddie and four others; Donovan, Jimmy, Will and Duke. I know their names because I've heard them talking to each other. It won't be the last time I see them. But as far as I know, there was no one else. At least, I never saw anyone else," Jack answered.

"So you saw them again?" Agent Travis said.

"I did. It didn't take them long to track me down. I had no car, no friends. I was cornered. I could only stay holed up in the motel for so long. I was an easy target," Jack said. "But it didn't come the way I expected."

"What do you mean?" Agent Travis asked.

"I mean, one morning I get a knock at the door. So I look out the window and there are three policemen and two squad cars in the lot. I opened the door. At first, I think they were taken back by the bruises and cuts on my face, but they start in by asking my name. I told them and soon enough they tackle me to the ground and tell me I am under arrest. I didn't hear the charge while I was busy being roughed up yet again. They weren't too happy with me and they let me feel it."

"What happened next?" Agent Travis asked, noticing in Jack's body language that this part of the conversation was making him uneasy. Travis thought, if all this is true, he sure hasn't had an easy life to this point, his sympathy for the young man growing.

"What happened next, Agent Travis," Jack said while shaking his head, "is I went to jail…for a long time. I sat in my cell for hours, unsure what was happening. Eventually the detective came in and started rattling off charges like he was unloading rounds. Discharging a firearm in public, damaging government property, intimidation, endangering the public, attempted murder of a police officer, you name it. They even said they heard I was a Communist. I didn't know what to do with that one."

Agent Travis' raised his brow in disbelief. "That isn't a good thing to be called these days," he said. "What on earth were they referring to with those charges?"

"I guess someone had fired on the police station in the middle of the night from the street and then run off. They had 'solid evidence' it was me. I can thank Fast Eddie and his gang for that. It didn't really matter though. With my recent arrival in town, brown skin, lack of means and my new found political affiliation, I wasn't going anywhere for a while. That is just what Eddie wanted. He told me so himself," Jack said.

"He told you so..." said Agent Travis, leading him further into the explanation.

"Yeah, a day or two goes by and I get a visitor. It's Eddie and company, come to say hi," Jack began. "I was in my cell and the four of them are standing outside of it. As the guard leaves us he tells Eddie to call for him if there is any trouble. How's that for ironic? Then Eddie does what Eddie does best, he starts talking. Asking me if I like the new place he had arranged for me, said it suited me. Told me how he was going to make my life a living hell. Went into great detail about it."

"So he chats me up for a while. I don't have anything to say to him. That is until he pulls out Tom's pocket watch, breathes on it with his foul breath and wipes it on his shirt, while giving me a wink. He says 'too bad daddy isn't here to save you,' real smug-like. This gets me off my bunk and over to the bars. I've had enough of this guy. I've had it with everything. I'm tired of being patient, of being stepped on, of being judged. I can't really explain it. I had just had enough."

"But what could you do?" Travis asked.

"Well Eddie comes close to the bars. He looks down the hall to make sure no one is watching, and is about to start talking again. Instead I surprise him with a right hand to the mouth, straight through the bars," Jack said as a smile expanded on Agent Travis' face.

Jack returned it with a smile of his own before continuing. "His head jerks back all awkward and he gets this wild look in his eyes. He goes to open his mouth again, to start cursing me out I'm sure, and I pop him a second time, even harder, right on his nose. This brings Donovan up to the bars and he reaches in for me. I slide back just in time to avoid his giant hand, which is swiping angrily at me."

Agent Travis can't contain himself and lets out a loud laugh. "Good for you, Jack," he said with pride. "Good for you."

"Yeah, it felt good, I won't lie, but it's short lived. I see Eddie's eyes have tear'd up from the blow to the nose. He stopped to wipe away a trickle of blood with a handkerchief. Then he says 'this dirty Spic seems to have forgotten what I can do to him…and his girl,' watching my face for a reaction. 'Yeah, that's right. I haven't forgotten about her.' I realize then I have to be careful."

"He motions me back to the bars. I reluctantly move forward. He grabs me by the shirt and pulls me close, the bars are the only space between us. We exchange words. He makes sure I understand him. Then he says 'we've got a job up in the Northwest that can't wait. It's going to take a few weeks. From what I hear, you're going to be here for a while. You did some bad stuff, kid. I wouldn't trade places with you for all the money in the Portland State bank. But we'll stop back when were done. Then you and I are going back to Logan to finish this. Think long and hard about that, boy. Otherwise, I'm going to bury you…and your girl…next to your pa'. That was it. They walked off," Jack said.

"Wait, Portland State bank. He said Portland State bank?" said Agent Travis, his mind searching. "That's what he said?"

"Yep," Jack replied, getting up now to stretch his legs.

"Portland State in Oregon was robbed this past winter," Agent Travis continued.

"Yep," Jack said again.

"You're suggesting Fast Eddie robbed that bank?" Agent Travis said, with his adrenaline driving again now.

"Nope, Eddie suggested it. I am just relaying it," Jack corrected him.

"An officer was killed in that shootout. That case is still open. No good leads either from what I hear. He'll go to Alcatraz for that," Travis said rhetorically.

While Agent Travis was thinking, Jack pulled a silver pocket watch out of his pocket and said, "It wasn't a total loss though. I was able to clip Tom's watch from Eddie while he was blathering in my ear up against the bars."

Jack held it up to admire it, enjoying a small moment of redemption, as Agent Travis looked on, wondering what could possibly come next.

11

After some quiet contemplation, Agent Travis regrouped and jumped back in with a different line of questioning, "Jack, this was what…last fall, right?"

"Yeah, this would have been pushing October by then," Jack said.

"And its September now. Have you been in jail this entire time?" Agent Travis asked.

"Until last week, that's where I was," Jack answered while looking away.

"How did you finally get out?" Travis asked.

"Over the months of questioning and meeting with the attorney, I began to wonder if I would ever get out. Their case was built on a strong eye witness account but not much else. Your guys from the FBI even came down once to talk about the communism thing, wanted to know my sources, or something stupid like that. I told them I wasn't communist but didn't tell them about anything else. Next I had a few court appearances too but none of it was going anywhere."

"Why not?" said Travis as he watched Jack who had returned to the ground and was now lying on his back. He looked as though he could use a break but Agent Travis decided there was a greater need to keep moving forward.

"Because of something called a continuance," Jack said, shaking his head in disgust as he stared in the branches above.

"Why did the judge grant a continuance?" Travis asked puzzled.

"Not one continuance, but several," Jack said. "Supposedly there was an eyewitness to my midnight shooting spree, but he was away on business. The prosecutor said this man's first-hand account would prove vital to the case and they couldn't proceed without him. I went to court three times and each time another one was granted."

"That does happen, Jack" Travis said somewhat apologetically.

"Doesn't seem right though that they can keep a man locked up for that long. I saw a lot of white men come and go from their cells and yet I remained."

Travis watched Jack look away. He could feel the hurt surfacing again in the young man stretched out before him. Travis didn't know what it was like to be treated differently due to the color of his skin but he knew it happened. He had seen it several times in law enforcement. Even the conversations he heard around the office showed there were still men that worked with a prejudice.

As Jack sat back up, Travis re-engaged him for the sake of lifting his spirits. "But you're out now and that's a good thing, right Jack?" Jack gave a slight nod, but otherwise sat motionless with his arms wrapped around his knees. "And how exactly did you manage to get out?"

Jack turned to Travis and said, "Two weeks ago, Eddie finally shows up. He and the gang come by again. Eddie tells me there were some 'unforeseen' complications up north and they had to escape up to Canada for a while. I had already read about the robbery in the paper, a botched armed robbery in the middle of the day with an officer killed in the shootout. It sounds like they didn't make off with very much. Fast Eddie put the blame squarely on Duke for dropping a bag with most of the money during the getaway. Eddie was real clear on how he dealt with him – two shells from his shotgun, one to kill him and another one for just the fun of it. At least that is how he said it," Jack said. "And Donovan was the one that fired the shot that killed the officer."

"He said that? About Donovan being the trigger man. He said that?" Agent Travis asked, anger percolating in his voice. "Why would he tell you that?"

"Because it's Fast Eddie. This guy can't shut up," Jack said. "Plus he knows I can't say anything because of Kate. He is constantly holding that over me. The way this guy talks though it's just a matter of time until his luck runs out."

"But with the last heist going awry, he's in a worse mood then normal.

Says the only thing that is going to make him feel better is watching me die. As it turns out, Duke was the supposed eye witness to my late night police station shootout. Eddie says Duke doesn't remember so well now that he's dead. He expects I will be released and he said he will be there to greet me. And if there are any complications this time, he would go after Kate instead," Jack said.

"When did they let you go?" Agent Travis said.

"Two days later I was scheduled to be processed and sent on my way," Jack said. "The plan was to release me on Wednesday morning. I spent the afternoon thinking about how I was going to get away from Eddie. He was sure to be waiting outside when the time came. But while I am laying on the bunk thinking about it, an officer comes by, unlocks my cell and walks me out to the lobby. Tells me I am free to go. Just like that, after nearly a year, I am free to go. No sorry, no nothing. Just get out."

"I would have been more upset about it but I knew it might be a blessing in disguise, seeing how Eddie wouldn't be expecting this. But still, before I step out of the police station lobby, I dug through my bag they handed me, looking for my gun, just in case. It was in there but there were no bullets. I wrapped it in my jacket anyway and cautiously made my way out of the station."

"Once outside I am looking every which way but as I had hoped there was no sign of Eddie, or the gang. I didn't want to wait around for them either so I walked real quick to the highway, thumbing for a ride. It didn't take long to get picked up and I was headed north, leaving the desert sunset in the rear view mirror. So while my exit from the lockup wasn't very ceremonious, at least I had a head start and needed to use that to my advantage to warn Kate. She had expected me back a long time ago," Jack said trailing off.

"Why didn't you call her while in jail?" Agent Travis said. "You could have let her know."

"I tried once. They gave me a phone call that first day in jail. It just didn't go as I had planned," Jack said.

"What does that mean?"

"It means the Sheriff's deputy put through the call to Kate's house. If it connected he was going to pass the phone through the bars. I was nervous. What was she going to think when she heard what had happened? I was kind of hoping she didn't answer," Jack said, more in the mode of thinking out loud, Travis noted.

"So, was there an answer?"

"There was," Jack continued. But it wasn't Kate. I could hear enough to know that it was her father. I remember my eyes dropping to the floor in embarrassment. I could only imagine what he was going to say to Kate about this. But it didn't go quite how I expected," Jack said dejectedly.

"How's that?" Travis answered.

"Well," Jack said with a sigh, in his uneasy manner, "The deputy introduced himself and asked for Kate. I heard some more talking. Then the deputy says my name, Jack Pepper. There was a pause, more talking on the other end of the phone, then the deputy says thank you and hangs up. Just like that, call's over."

Agent Travis remained silent as Jack looked over with pained eyes. Travis was now beginning to trust Jack. The pain that exuded from his words in moments like this could only come from someone who had lived, or was still living, a tragedy. He gave Jack the time he needed to continue.

"Deputy turns and says there was no Kate there, and the man didn't know who I was. Asked if I have the right number. I didn't respond. I knew it was right. I went over to the bunk and lay down, staring at the ceiling. Kate's father was nearly 400 miles away, yet I could see the smug smile he must have had on his face with that one," Jack said, obviously still hurt by the thought.

Travis waited for the pain to subside before asking, "Have you talked to her then? You've obviously been back a few days."

"I tried. I went to see her the first night I was back. Last Wednesday I guess. I went to her house and I saw her, Trigger too," Jack said.

"What did she say?" Agent Travis asked.

"Don't know. Didn't talk to her," Jack answered, staring ahead blankly.

Flabbergasted, Travis' frustration took over. "Jack, what you are doing doesn't make sense," he said as he got up, annoyed by this man and his lack of getting help when he needed it most. Was he too proud, too stupid or too blind to see it? Agent Travis walked a few steps away to think, turning his back on Jack in disgust.

It was past 2 pm now. Agent Travis knew it was time to make the call. He stood with his hands on his hips, thinking. Should he put Jack back in hand-cuffs and haul him to Salt Lake to sort this whole thing out? It was an all too appealing option. But what if Jack wasn't lying? What if the story was true? That would mean Fast Eddie and company would soon be here, if they weren't already. What would happen to the mysterious Kate if he left with Jack? Was he willing to risk her life, and take away her future, if he was wrong?

He closed his eyes and tried to form a picture of her in his mind, even though he didn't know what she looked like, as he recalculated all the information he knew to this point. The story was extreme and lacking physical evidence, but it could possibly be corroborated with some follow-up interviews. Jack seemed to know the details, without hesitation, which is usually an indication of the truth. In the end, it would come down to trust. Was Jack someone that he could trust?

The answer came with a click. Agent Travis knew what it meant before he turned around. Jack had pulled his gun, and cocked the trigger. In an instant, Travis' mind went into a frenzy, rapidly processing every piece of information he had heard today. He was looking for something to use, knowing that in this situation, his mind would be a better weapon than his gun. He turned slowly towards Jack, with both hands raised from his sides, and his heart banging against his chest wall, and said humbly, "Jack, I'm sure…"

"Quiet!" Jack whispered loudly, staring off past Agent Travis, whose eyes had gone to Jack's gun, which was drawn but pointing straight down into the ground.

Realizing that Jack wasn't threatening him, he looked back over his shoulder in the direction Jack was staring. Sure enough, on the opposite ridge line, were two men, one of whom was holding what appeared to be a shotgun across his arms. It was difficult to tell at that distance, but it sure looked like these men were watching Jack and Agent Travis.

"Who is that?" Travis asked in a whisper.

"Can't tell from this far out," Jack said, without taking his eyes off the men.

Agent Travis put his hands down and glanced back to Jack. He noticed a steely look in his eye that he hadn't seen before. Jack's youthful face hardened with focus. It was the kind of look a man gets when he's out to protect himself, and his family.

"Maybe we should go," Agent Travis said cautiously, not to provoke the situation.

"Maybe you should go," Jack said resolutely, unflinching.

They stood in silence for several seconds before Jack pulled his eyes away from Agent Travis and stepped into the direction of the woods.

"We're not done yet, Jack" Agent Travis said loudly, moving his hand to his own firearm concealed inside his jacket as he stepped to cross Jack's path, holding out his other palm to signal Jack to stop.

Jack stopped and looked down at the ground. Agent Travis studied him closely, while considering his next move.

It was Jack whose demeanor softened just enough to end the crisis. He shifted his weight to the other foot and said, without ever looking up, "You're right. We aren't done yet. You need to find Kate. She needs someone to protect her while I finish this." Jack looked up before slowly beginning to step away.

Agent Travis looked back at the men on the ridge and then to Jack before pulling his hand back out of his jacket, knowing this wasn't the time for ultimatums.

"Jack," Agent Travis said in a more gentle tone now, "you don't have to do this. We can find a better way."

Jack stopped after a few more steps and turned to face him, "Things still come down to right and wrong. They may not always be black and white, but they are right and wrong. Remember that Agent Travis."

And with that Travis watched Jack as he turned, and with haste, started up the mountain towards the trees in the exact manner he had come down earlier that morning. The confidence in his stride gave Agent Travis hope that he might actually see Jack alive again.

PART II

12

Kate stared out the window of the formal dining room into the backyard where she watched Trigger chase a chipmunk through the tall grass. Trigger had crept in range of the poor creature before breaking out in a full sprint. Once spotted, the chipmunk darted for his nearby burrow. Trigger gave chase but didn't catch it. It was all play to him. She had never seen him catch one, either due to their cunning or his big heart, she thought.

Her reflection in the window caught her eye and drew it away from the scene outside. She had recently turned twenty-one. Her appearance hadn't changed much from the day she met Jack. She still had fair skin, straight brown hair parted in the middle, resting behind her ears and traveling down to the middle of her back, and even a few freckles remained from those earlier days. But despite those similarities, she was now clearly defined as a woman, and turned heads everywhere she went.

She was, however, indifferent to that kind of attention. Given her age and the fact that she resided in Utah meant she was at a prime age to marry. She wasn't oblivious to that expectation and looked forward to that day, but when it came to her choices, it was still Jack or everyone else. Despite her best efforts to move on at her family's insistence, she had trouble doing so. If only she knew what had become of him, and if he would ever return as he promised, maybe she could have closure. But since that hope was fading more each day, she had been forcing herself to at least review her options. After all, if she waited much longer, she knew the best of her alternatives would begin to disappear to marriages of their own.

Kate brought her hand up to the window and traced his name with her finger, thinking hard about what she should do next.

Kate had been attending Utah State Agricultural College for the past year. The school was located at the base of Logan Canyon, not far from her family's home, which allowed her to live with them while going to school. This gave her access to the campus life, and new friends, but also allowed her to get away at the end of each day, an excuse she used with some regularity to avoid dating. But it was a fine line to walk. She craved having an education and being involved but by doing so, she attracted more attention than she currently wanted. As time passed, she felt those defensive walls crumbling down. She was now at the point where she began accepting offers from the 'everyone else' contingent.

Near the top of that list was her long-time friend, Billy Hendricks. They had met not long after she met Jack. Once school had begun, Kate was placed in a desk next to Billy. She and Billy hit it off right away, talking about his father's land and how she had been up there a few times with Jack. From there the conversations flowed easily and often. Billy was quick to notice her cheery personality and unselfish nature, and it didn't take long for him to form a crush. Over the course of that year they became good friends, giving them a foundation to build from in later years.

As they got older, Kate maintained that friendship with Billy, although any time spent with a boy outside of class was primarily limited to Jack. Billy noticed, as did her friends, who teased her relentlessly about being in love with a brown boy. She didn't mind at all. The color of his skin paled in comparison to her enjoyment of being with him. She recognized Jack was quiet at school but when the two of them were together in the canyons, he was a different person. Sometimes she wondered if he saved every thought just to share them with her. The quiet, loner Jack that existed in the rest of the world was a stranger to her.

Billy, however, did mind and made it point to take subtle jabs whenever he could, whether about Jack or to him directly. This jealousy must have built up inside Billy until it finally boiled over one day after school during their freshman year.

The story goes that Jack had stumbled upon Billy and his friends smoking behind the school, an activity that had been clearly communicated would not be tolerated on school grounds. Knowing that Jack might say something to Kate, who would certainly disapprove, he confronted Jack. Jack did what he does best and said nothing while Billy raged on about him, serving up every insult that came to mind. Jack's silence only served to provoke Billy further, who decided it was time to teach Jack who the better man was. With a brisk upper-cut to Jack's chin, the fight was on.

Jack hadn't been oblivious to Billy's interest in Kate but he found it as a mild inconvenience instead of a serious threat. He knew where he stood with Kate and she never gave him any reason to think otherwise. But if this was going to happen (and there was no way out of it now), he sure wasn't going to let Kate hear that he lost in a fight to Billy.

Being dazed by the quick strike, Jack retreated a few steps to get his bearings. Billy had the size advantage and he pursued after Jack, swinging wildly in the process with his friends cheering him on. Jack kept his head about him, blocking and dogging as he retreated. He began to circle around on his backwards walk, letting Billy punch himself out in the process. Once back to where they started, Jack planted his back foot and lunged forward, shoving Billy in the chest with both hands, and then struck him with a blow to the right cheek.

This startled Billy, unaware that Jack had any fight in him, but it didn't dissuade him. He continued after Jack to reward him with what he thought was a well-deserved pummeling. The fight continued as it had before with Billy coming forward and Jack moving in reverse. After another full circle back to the beginning, Jack cemented his back foot again and pushed forward with the same motion of pushing and then popping, again to the right side of Billy's face.

With that second punch, Billy's eyes grew large. He cursed up a storm before lunging at Jack with his full fury on display. Jack jumped to the side avoiding Billy's grasp. As Billy flew by, Jack punched him hard in the side of the head, hitting him squarely in the ear, causing Billy to lose his balance and fall face first to the ground. Jack was quick to capitalize by jumping on Billy's back and holding his face against the ground. With his arms pinned to his side by Jack's legs, Billy was unable to get free.

As Jack was contemplating how much punishment to inflict, he was tackled from behind by one of Billy's friends and sent tumbling, before coming to rest against the side of the building. With Billy now free and his friends at his side, Jack began to look for an escape. With all routes blocked, he stood up, dusted himself off and stared defiantly at Billy, waiting for the fight to resume.

But as the story goes, there would be no more punches. Ms. Ford, the school's history teacher, heard the commotion and had come out to see what all the ruckus was about, her presence on the scene immediately putting an end to the extra-curricular activity.

Jack hadn't mention it to Kate but she heard all about it from her friends, and the bruise on Billy's face the next day confirmed the account she had been told. Given that Jack didn't say anything about it, Kate decided not to either. After all, there was no sense inciting a further rivalry between them.

Regardless of what had happened that day years ago, it had long since been forgiven. Billy was also attending Utah State and had matured like most boys do. She knew he was interested in her based on his repeated invitations and despite turning him down several times previously, she had finally agreed to a date.

Their first date was not even a month ago. He had taken her to the Bluebird restaurant on Main Street. The Bluebird was already an iconic establishment in Cache valley by 1954, having opened at their current location in 1923; their courage and quality having survived the great depression. Now with the economy prospering, the tables were full and the wait long so they decided to eat at the bar. Despite a substantial menu, they settled on the staple of most college students; burgers and fries. After all, despite her refinement, Kate was never much more than a country girl at heart.

Following dinner, he took her to see Hitchcock's new movie, Rear Window, starring Jimmy Stewart and Grace Kelly which was playing at the theater in downtown Logan. She didn't care for scary movies but she reluctantly agreed to squelch Billy's insistence. And as expected, during the course of the movie she found several scenes frightening, which made it necessary to hold Billy's arm, or sometimes his hand. Her epiphany came with the ease and comfort in doing so. Maybe she could find love in someone other than Jack, she had thought.

Later that night when back at home, lying in her bed recollecting on the evening, she decided maybe her family was right, that it was time to move on. She swore in her heart to at least give Billy a chance.

As she starred out the window at Trigger that afternoon, it had now been several dates, including the moment they shared their first kiss in their stable behind her house last week, ironically in almost the same spot she had kissed Jack goodbye. It had been a sweet moment but one that had since turned against her. She figured it would help make her forget Jack but instead, he was still there, in the back of her mind, her feelings for him stronger than ever. It was becoming a point of frustration. Something would have to give soon.

"Where are you?" she spoke softly to no one but herself, closing her eyes while leaning her forehead against the window pane. She felt the cool glass on her skin as her mind searched through pictures of him. They were becoming harder to recall. She clutched the curtains in vain, hoping it would help her remember better. It didn't.

Before she could wrench them further, a sudden knock came at the front door. She lifted her head in surprise and turned to look, not realizing her question was about to be answered.

13

Agent Travis had been sitting in his car across the street from the Austin home for the past ten minutes, reviewing notes from his conversation with Jack. It hadn't taken long to get Kate's address. Logan was a friendly town. He needed only to ask a few people downtown and, since he looked respectable in a suit and tie, he was easily pointed in the right direction.

But before driving back up the gradual slope on the east side of town, he had driven back into town, anxious to phone this one in. He called the direct line to the FBI Operator and asked for the Special Agent in Charge, his supervisor, Agent Anderson.

"This is Agent Anderson," the man spoke after the line connected.

"Agent Anderson, I am glad I caught you. It's Travis."

"Travis, where have you been all day?" Anderson said, mildly irritated.

"In Logan, sir, following a lead on the Cache County Bank robbery case," Agent Travis said.

There was a hesitation before Agent Anderson continued, "Well…"

Travis felt a bit of comfort in his boss's directness after a day of having to draw information out of Jack. "Well sir, I interviewed a person of interest. He seems to know a lot the case. He gave me quite a story. I need to follow-up on this lead but I was thinking about arranging for back-up."

"Why? Are you in danger?" Anderson said, his voice devoid of any real concern, almost as if he was making casual conversation.

The response set Travis back on his heels. He wasn't in imminent danger but he felt some concern for his safety, and had hoped his boss would pick up on that. Eventually, he replied, "No, I don't believe so."

"Good," Agent Anderson replied swiftly. "Then get back to work. We could use some good news on this one. When will you be back?"

"Tomorrow," Travis said, resigning his fate to going it alone for the rest of the evening.

They exchanged good-byes and the line went dead.

Travis held the receiver, knowing there was one more call that had to be made. He contemplated the task at hand. He was nervous to tell his wife that he might be staying overnight. It wasn't that she couldn't manage on her own, but he thought she may be able to detect the emotions fused in his voice. He knew he was on to something and he didn't want to excite her with the possibility that he may have cracked the case, nor did he want to alarm her with the reality of the danger. It would take the full extent of his training to fool his spouse, something that was hard to do given she knew him better than he knew himself.

After shoring up his composure, he picked up the phone and dialed home. Luckily, Sarah was there.

"Sarah," Travis said when his wife said hello.

"Hi Honey," she answered back. "How's your day going?"

It was then that he realized he needed to hear her voice, feeling drained after a full day of field work. "Not bad," he said, working his best nonchalant tone. "It's been productive. Had a good interview and now heading to do another."

"Another?" she said concerned. "Does that mean you will be getting home late?"

"Or possibly tomorrow. It's hard to say," he told her. "Like I said, it's been a productive day and I need to keep working. Will you be ok? Do you need anything?" the last two questions coming one right after the other in an overly aggressive manner. He grimaced hoping she didn't pick up on that.

After a moment of silence, Sarah said, "Yes, I will be ok and no, I don't need anything." If she had noticed, she didn't let on. "Will you call me later and let me know your plans?"

"Yes Sweetheart, absolutely," Travis responded, knowing he may have missed the mark in fooling his wife. "Good-bye then," he said as he started to put the phone down.

"Honey," Sarah said at the last second.

Agent Travis put the phone back up to his ear and said, "Yes," as patiently as he could.

"I love you," she replied.

That caught Travis off guard. They had never been one of those couples to say that in public and here he was standing at a pay phone on Main St. Nevertheless, the words ran him through and he didn't want to leave them hanging out there with no response. He looked around to make sure no one could hear him. "I love you too," he said.

He hung up the phone, a modest smile crossing his face, as he headed around to the driver's side of the car, ready for the short journey to Kate's house.

He was still reminiscing about it as he sat in the parked car next to the Austin home, studying his notes. He looked down at his watch. It was a quarter to 4 p.m. Time to get back to work, Travis closed his notebook. He exited the car and made his way up to the door, surveying the scene as he went. The house was well kept. No cars were in the driveway. The neighborhood had a few people milling about but overall it was quiet. He concluded this wasn't likely to be a dangerous encounter.

Within seconds of his knock, the door swung open and he immediately recognized the young woman in front of him. Despite the limited description from Jack, he knew this must be Kate. He quickly launched into his pre-scripted lines.

"Miss, my name is Agent Travis. I am with the FBI. I am looking to speak with Kate Austin. Is she here?" Agent Travis said, holding out his badge while watching her reaction, wondering if she would start the interview with a lie.

"Oh," she said startled. "Why yes, I am Kate Austin."

That went well, Travis thought, as he stared at her, forgetting that he still had his badge up and that she was waiting for him to speak. Embarrassed, he regrouped, "Good. Well. If I may..." Travis said clumsily as he motioned to come inside.

"Why, of course." Kate said with a hesitant laugh. "Where's my manners. I just wasn't expecting this. Yes, please come in."

Agent Travis stepped into the foyer and was guided into the living room. He noted the modern, clean look of the room. Whoever had decorated it had a refined taste. It was obvious from both the interior and exterior of the home that the Austin's were careful with their image.

"Please be seated Agent Travis. May I get you anything? A lemonade perhaps?" Kate said.

"Yes, thank you," Agent Travis said, glad to have something to combat the dehydration he was feeling after a day in the sun.

Kate walked into the kitchen, the sound of glass and ice colliding, shooing away the silence. When she returned she handed Agent Travis the glass before sitting down across from him. He noted she had on a red and black plaid dress with sleeves that came to her elbows and a matching belt wrapped about her waist. Travis had pictured a girl in blue jeans with a rugged outdoor look from the stories of exploring canyons but that wasn't the case. The young lady who sat across from him had a certain refinement that came with a proper upbringing, but it was tempered by a kind and humble look coming from her eyes. Her eyes were trying to mask the obvious nerves she felt due to the circumstance but Agent Travis could see it nonetheless.

Kate was sitting rather far out onto the edge of her seat, obviously anxious to hear what this is all about. After a long drink that exhausted nearly all of the contents of the glass, Agent Travis put the cup down and sat forward, ready to go to work.

"Miss Austin," he started before she interrupted.

"Kate is fine," she said with a half-hearted smile.

"Kate, when was the last time you saw Jack Pepper?"

Her countenance dimmed slightly. She looked down and smoothed out her dress on her lap before looking up and saying, "About a year ago, I guess."

"Has he tried to contact you since then?" Agent Travis said.

"No," Kate answered dispirited.

"Have you tried to contact him?" Travis continued.

"No. I wouldn't know how. I don't know where he's gone," Kate said.

"Really?" Travis said with counterfeit surprise. "I understood you two to be friends."

"Well yes, that is true," she said, searching carefully for her words, "but all the same, I don't know where he is," as she turned her eyes away from Agent Travis' stare.

"Well I do," he said back with a straight face and a tone void of emotion. There it is, he thought. Where was that when I was talking to my Sarah?

Kate stood up slowly and walked to the front window. Travis could see her discomfort and now felt bad for being more FBI than human. This wasn't a suspect he reminded himself and decided to dial it down a notch.

"Kate, what I meant to say was, I know where Jack is and he asked me to come here. He thought you might be in danger and I came to see if I can help."

With her back turned to Agent Travis, she reached up to wipe away a tear, before earnestly asking, "How is he?"

"He looked just fine to me," Agent Travis said, doing his best to be reassuring. "He seemed like a guy who could take care of himself but he wanted to make sure you were safe."

This reassurance brought Kate away from the window and back to her chair. She sat down again, waiting for Agent Travis to continue.

"I spoke with Jack at length this morning," Travis said.

"Jack's in Logan!" Kate blurted out, rising from her chair once again, with a dumbfounded look in her eyes. Her mouth hung open, while her eyes were searching for understanding.

"I spoke with him this morning," Agent Travis started to say again, signaling for her to sit. "In Logan, yes. We talked for a long while. He told me quite a story. What I need is for you to confirm what he told me. Can you do that? It's very important that you leave nothing out. That is the best way I can help Jack and protect you."

Agent Travis watched Kate closely, her mouth still hanging open, staring back in his direction but right through him. He waited before motioning again to the chair and she slowly sank down into it.

After taking a minute for herself, she said, "That could take a while."

"I understand," Agent Travis said. "If your parents are home, it might be better if they were to join us?"

"They're not here. My mother has gone up to visit my sister in Soda Springs and my father has a board meeting tonight at the hospital," Kate said. "He won't be home until after dark."

"I would certainly understand if you wanted to wait for him, but…" Travis trailed off with a concerned look.

"But what?" Kate hastily asked, taking the bait.

"But," Agent Travis said awkwardly, not looking to cause alarm, "I think our time is limited. It may be in Jack's best interest for us to talk now."

At hearing those words, Kate took a deep breath, holding it for an extra measure, before letting it out and saying with a firm resolve, "Alright then Agent Travis, what would you like to know?"

Knowing that a mutual understanding had been reached, Travis flipped open his notebook, pulled out a pencil and looked up at Kate. Although he was anxious to start at the end, he knew it was best to get a story from the beginning.

"How about you tell me what happened in the canyon that day when you and Jack went riding? I would like to make sure I understand that," Agent Travis said.

Kate looked down at her dress again. "Alright Agent Travis," she began, "but in order to understand it, I am going to have to start a little farther back, if that is ok with you?"

"Whatever it takes to find the truth will be just fine," Travis said.

With that, Kate stood again and walked back over to the window, collecting her thoughts. Agent Travis leaned back on the sofa. Obviously, getting her to remain seated was a lost cause that he would no longer try to enforce.

After a long delay, Travis said, "Kate" before being cut-off as she finally spoke.

"I will tell you the truth, Agent Travis, but only as I see it. From there you will have to make up your own mind about the truth. Can we agree on that?"

With a slight nod of the head, Agent Travis said, "Let's begin."

14

Agent Travis watched as the afternoon light shone through the window and landed on Kate, her fair skin glowing with a translucent quality. She gently pushed her hair behind her ear in an unconscious motion and stood with her arms folded, her natural beauty evident in the silhouette. Travis understood why she and Jack meant so much to each other. Both had a humility and kindness that radiated in who they were. When one spoke of the other, their countenance brightened as their feelings filled the air.

"Agent Travis, are you familiar with the mining that was done in Cache County back at the turn of the century?" Kate said, still looking out the window.

This caught Agent Travis by surprise. He put his pencil down while thinking about the question. "No, I don't believe I have heard that before," he said. His gaze stayed locked on Kate while he worked to figure out her angle.

"It was quite robust really. There are some two dozen mines or so between Brigham City and Bear Lake. La Plata, Blue Bell, Moon, Honey Bee, the Amazon, Spring Hollow. Like I said, there were many."

She cleared her voice like a college professor preparing for a lecture and then continued, "You wouldn't know it to look at them but these mountains have all kinds of treasures. They mined out gold, silver, zinc, lead, calcium, copper. You name it. It was a productive mining area from 1880 to about 1920. It brought people from all over the country. Some did quite well, others not. In the end though, it wasn't productive enough. The claims were abandoned and the mining companies moved on to other mountains. Those miners that stayed behind turned into farmers or ranchers."

"But in moving on, those companies left a lot in terms of history up in those mountains. Nothing of value really but enough to keep a couple kids busy exploring. That was part of our canyon adventure. We brought flashlights with us in case we came across a mine shaft or a cave. It was the thrill of what we might find. I found it a bit frightening to go into the dark, into the unknown, but not Jack. He was always so confident and reassuring. If he could tell I was nervous, he would hold my hand and promise me that we would make it out safely. That always got me," Kate said with a smile. "I don't know if it was because I knew he would do what he said or I just liked it when we held hands, probably both."

"How old were you?" Travis interjected.

"It's been ever since we met, twelve years old I guess," Kate said.

Agent Travis continued writing as Kate continued her story.

"Summers were the best of times for us. We spent a few days a week up in the canyon. Green Canyon was our favorite and not just because we could walk there but because of all that canyon has to offer; caves, views, old structures, the Spring Hollow mine, a mountain valley full of sheep and cattle, and a stream running through the middle of it. We spent a lot of time there, especially on William Hendricks' land. He owns quite a bit of it up there. It was all sacred to us. We treated it like our kingdom, where Jack and I were the rulers."

"Jack always knew the mines better than I did though. He was more daring, willing to go to the end of each run to see where they went. Spring Hollow mine was his favorite. It is a drift mine," Kate explained before being interrupted.

"I'm sorry…a drift mine?" Agent Travis asked as he peered out from behind his notebook.

"Oh, yes, the kind that you can enter horizontally, straight into the mountain, versus a shaft mine where you drop straight down, or a slope mine or an open pit. Most of the ones up here are drift or slope mines. They were sealed up when the miners pulled out but that didn't stop us. Jack would bring a hammer or crow bar to take care of that. One way or another we always found our way in," Kate said.

"He loved the Spring Hollow mine. It was so intricate. There are tunnels and adits and ventilation shafts going every which way. He gave them all names. It even had multiple levels that ran from slope to slope, with rooms of all sizes left from the excavation. It made the exploration all the more interesting, the idea that we may find something long forgotten, or hidden. I don't think I ever got to see all of it though," Kate said trailing off.

"Why not?" Agent Travis said.

Fidgeting, Kate answered, "We were up there one day, when we were sixteen, and Jack and I entered the mine like we usually do. It was a hot, summer day and the cool air of the mine was a welcome relief for a change. Jack convinced me to play a game of hide-and-seek in the west side of the mine. I felt like being a sport so I agreed, even though I still wasn't all that comfortable in the mine alone. But I had my flashlight so we set out to play. We decided that I would go to hide and Jack would come look for me. I made my way as deep as I dared, to a large cavernous room at the end of a descending trail and turned off my light to wait for him," Kate said before pausing.

"Have you ever been in a mine, Agent Travis?"

Travis stopped writing momentarily as he searched his thoughts. "I can't say that I have," he answered.

"Well, it's beyond any darkness you can imagine. You can put your hand right in front of your face and not see a thing. It's cold too, and lifeless. It can be an eerie thing to sit alone in the cold dark of a mine. After only a few minutes, I had enough and went to turn on my flashlight. But as I went to push up the switch, I dropped it. I heard the glass lens break on impact with the rocks."

Agent Travis watched as Kate's countenance changed. Her voice remained calm but her eyes emitted a distinct dread, as if she was still in the darkness.

"I felt around on the ground for my flashlight, being careful not to cut myself. Once I found it, I pushed up on the switch and nothing happened. The bulb had broken too. I kept pushing the switch up and down in vain, my fear of the dark swelling around me. I immediately started calling for Jack but he didn't respond. I thought he would be close enough and I would instantly hear his footsteps but he wasn't. I didn't know where he was. It was the darkest, scariest thing I had ever experienced," she said, taking a deep breath to keep her composure intact.

"I tried to remember how I had gotten to that room, but I had gone a long ways and my mind panicked. I probably should have just sat there and kept calling for Jack. He would have found me soon enough but instead I did the opposite. I stopped yelling and started crawling my way out. I did this for what seemed like an eternity. At times I would stop to call out, or cry, but none of it helped and before long I was sure I was lost for good," Kate said as she paced slowly around the room.

"Finally, as I sat on the ground, leaning up against the tunnel wall, I said a quiet prayer, hoping God would hear me. Then I waited. I remember thinking He may not even be able to hear me from down there. But not long after my prayer, I heard the faint sound of Jack calling my name. I shouted back to him. Gradually, his yelling got closer and closer until I could see his light coming. I knew I was saved. I hugged that boy like I was never letting go," she said with a laugh.

"He led me out. I had my face buried in his neck the whole way up to the surface, his arm wrapped tight around me. We walked out into the warm light of the sun. I felt like I had been saved in so many ways. I cried again, couldn't stop for some reason. Jack was patient with me. We went to the stream and sat for a while. Then we talked. We had the best conversations, Jack and I, like we were meant to always be together," Kate said, looking at Agent Travis' face for understanding.

Agent Travis, feeling uncomfortable by the personal direction the conversation had taken, looked away and asked the only question that he could think of to ask, "Did you ever go into the mine again?"

"No, I never did. Not that one, not any. My days as a miner ended like most of the others; big hopes but left with nothing but a story. That was ok with me. Jack could do enough exploring for both of us."

"I did get one treasure though," Kate said, finally sitting again. "That day, walking home, just before we hit the base of the canyon, Jack stopped. I turned back to ask what was a matter and he reached out, and pulled me close to him. We were face-to-face, holding each other. He gently touched the side of my face, and then he kissed me. Never said a word, just kissed me. It was our first kiss. It turned out to be one of the best days of my life."

Agent Travis had watched Kate closely, her light both shining and dimming at the same time when she talked about Jack. He could see those feelings were still strong but concluded she was mostly suffering from their time apart. No wonder she had jumped when hearing he was in town.

None of this, however, had anything to do with the story Jack had told him earlier and daylight was wasting. He wondered if Jack had already found another hard spot with the mysterious men. It was then he realized the pace of his interview was too slow, and he was letting the interviewee dictate the terms. If he was going to help Jack and solve this case, he would have to be more persistent in his questioning.

"Kate, you and Jack are evidently very fond of each other, but I am here to investigate a bank robbery. I don't see how this is at all relevant," Agent Travis said.

Kate stood up once again and walked back to her spot at the window. Parting the curtains to see outside, she said, "I am surprised you can't see it. Why these men are pursuing Jack…what they want."

She paused as his mind spun.

"It's not just about revenge. Once you work that out, it becomes even more obvious why I am telling you about the mine."

Agent Travis stayed locked on Kate, glued to her every word. He looked down at his notebook and flipped back through a couple of pages. Now seeing the clues in a different light, he began to put the pieces together.

"It's not that Jack is a bad person, quite the opposite. He is misunderstood. What motivates him is different than you or I," Kate continued.

It suddenly dawned on him how the pieces fit. He couldn't believe he had missed it. He dropped his pencil into the notebook and hung his head in disappointment. He knew what Kate was about to say before she even said it. All that was left was the sting of the words as they left her mouth.

Kate turned and looked directly at him as she said it, "The mine is where Jack hid the money."

15

Could it really have been that obvious? Agent Travis thought. He felt his face become flush and hot. He had spent the entire day with Jack and not been able to make this conclusion on his own. It did make sense. Fast Eddie had been laid up in a hospital for months according to Jack. If Jack had told the authorities, Eddie would have easily been found. Eddie must have known that. Since no one came after him, he could have chosen to move on versus risking a return to Logan. Even if he did want revenge, that could have been accomplished with a single bullet and not this extended game of cat-and-mouse. No, the only reason Jack was still alive is because he had something Eddie wanted.

Agent Travis got up from his chair and paced around the room, now becoming the one unable to sit. Kate stood motionless by the window, allowing him to work through the details. His frustration had overcome his ability to think clearly. He started to speak on multiple occasions, but stopped, not wanting to compound the problem with unproductive comments. After a while he decided to skip ahead and ask what he really wanted to know, "Kate, where is Jack?"

"You're the one that has seen him, Agent Travis, not me," Kate said calmly.

"That doesn't mean I know where he is. You're his girlfriend. You must know where he is," Travis said.

"Am I?" she said. "I certainly don't feel like a girlfriend. It has been almost a year since I last saw him, or talked to him."

"Still, you can help him now. You can bring him back. Jack has been mostly lucky to this point but right now he is out-numbered and has limited resources. You can help him by telling me where he is!" Agent Travis said adamantly while pounding his hand on the top of the sofa.

Kate, arms still folded under her chest, gave it some thought before replying, "Jack knows how to take care of himself. He's smarter than you know. He will come find me when he is ready, when we're safe."

Agent Travis stared back at Kate, astonished. The resolute look on her face told him that was the end of the discussion. She must be as hard-headed as Jack, Travis thought. Since she wasn't going to be offering up any information on how to find Jack, he would have to find another way to locate him.

But that would have to wait. For now, there was still more work to be done here. Seeing how Kate could be considered an accomplice if Jack did have the money, he decided to continue on with his interview.

Travis took a deep breath, regaining his composure. "Would you mind telling me what happened that day in the canyon when you were taken to the hideout?" he said with a look meant to elicit the full truth.

She walked back to the chair and sat down. Agent Travis took this as an acceptance of her offer to continue to help. Her eyes turned soft and bright as she began, "It was an anniversary day."

"An anniversary day?" Travis asked, moving back to the sofa and picking up his notebook.

"Yes, three years together, exclusively," she replied with a smile. "We love to celebrate; birthdays, anniversaries for all sorts of things, we even made up holidays. It was all just a reason to go spend the day together. I would pack food to take with us, and a blanket for a picnic. I would prepare different meals each time, trying to surprise him with something special for dessert; chocolate cake, homemade caramels or pineapple upside-down cake…that was Jack's favorite."

"He came over around 9 am that day, if I remember right, and went directly to the stable. He didn't come up to the house much anymore," Kate said while looking down uneasily, her tone and demeanor adjusting to each part of the story.

"That morning he went in to bridle and saddle the horses. When I came out to join him, I saw that he had picked Bridget and Sunset. That made me happy. Bridget and Sunset took to following each other around constantly, almost like they had their own obsession with each other. They were obviously in love and I liked when we went out on them together. Jack knew that," her face beaming now.

"It took over an hour to ride to the top of Green Canyon that day. We went up through Hyde Park and into Birch Canyon. We didn't mind the extended ride. Birch is lovely, full of wonderful views. It was nice riding together. Eventually we got to the top and came over the ridge, dropping down into the valley at the top of Green Canyon. We tied up Bridget and Sunset at the place we wanted to come back for lunch and then set out on foot. We had been hiking on the trail for a while when we came around a corner and ran into a man coming out of the bushes."

"Fast Eddie" Agent Travis said rhetorically.

"Who's Fast Eddie?" Kate said bewildered.

Agent Travis paused, realizing that would be the first time she has heard that name. "Oh, the leader of the gang, the man who assaulted you," he said, before realizing that wasn't the best choice of words. Seeing that had made Kate uncomfortable, he offered an apologetic "sorry" before quickly moving on. "Please continue where you left off."

"Well, he looked afraid at first and then he got angry. He came at us with gun drawn. It was frightening but I assumed it was a misunderstanding that we could easily explain. Unfortunately, he wouldn't let us do any talking. He told us to keep quiet and marched us off the trail and through a field. I saw where we were headed, towards the old miner's cabin. I hadn't been inside there for quite a while. It was nothing more than boards for walls, a few small windows, a wooden plank front porch and a roof that looked ready to cave in."

"Once inside, he cuffed Jack to the stove and sent me to the other side of the room, to sit on the bed," Kate said while averting her eyes from Agent Travis. "Then he accused us of following him on purpose and started in about the bank robbery. He seemed especially proud about it," she said emphasizing it for effect.

"What did he say? Is there anything specific that you can remember? It will be a big help in sorting this all out," Travis asked.

"I don't recall all of it as my mind was racing," Kate said. "But he told us how they entered through a man hole into an underground tunnel from the sewer during the night. It connected to some other doors and then into a boiler room, which was in the bank. Once inside they had the bank all to themselves. Eddie sent a man up to the lobby to watch the street while they worked."

"Apparently, the vault door was an older model and they used a cutting torch to get through it. He called the bank fools for not using a door with some copper. I guess the torch wouldn't work then or something. It took them all of twenty minutes to cut through it, he said. Anyway, once inside the vault, they took out several bags of money, two of which were very large and heavy. He had those with him in the hideout."

"After they finished clearing out the money, they went back out through the tunnel door and relocked it so no one would know how they did it. They even shot out a window as they drove away to make it look like they came in from the lobby. He was very satisfied with his work. He said he was the best when it came to breaking into places."

Agent Travis rubbed his temples. It all added up; the access to the vault, the bullet holes inside the bank lobby, across from the broken window. Some of the details Kate provided were known only by those close to the case. The combined story from Jack and Kate would allow him to offer a whole new theory on the robbery when he returned to the Bureau. He made sure to capture as much as he could in his notebook, the words being pressed into the paper with needless force.

"Then what did he do?" Travis asked.

"Then he attacked us," Kate said, now visibly nervous. She smoothed her dress in her lap again as her eyes began to tear up. Travis handed her a handkerchief which she accepted before continuing.

"He hit Jack first, broke his nose, and then he came after me. He is very strong, and very mean. He said many things I won't repeat. I fought him off the best I could. I really don't remember much after that, except for thinking he would eventually kill me. When I heard the gunshots I assumed that was it; that I was dead, ready to wake up in the next life. It's a memory you don't soon forget." Kate stopped smoothing out her dress and began working over the handkerchief in her hands.

"Then I saw Jack's face above me and figured he must be dead too. I thought it was fitting that we could go together. It was only when I grabbed his hand and he winced that I started to realize we were still alive," relief coming over her face with the memory.

"Jack urged me to get up but I was having trouble standing, and focusing. He put his arm around me and helped me up. I looked over and saw this Eddie lying face down on the fireplace, bleeding. I never saw him move. Jack had somehow beaten him. We left him there dead and stumbled out the front door, headed across the field to the trail."

"We hadn't gone far when I needed to stop. My head was aching. I thought I was going to be sick. Jack helped me off the trail and down behind some bushes. I laid my head on the ground to stop the world from spinning. It felt like only a few moments before Jack was trying to get me up again. But when I looked up, I saw that he had both large, black bags from the hideout, one over each shoulder. He must have gone back for them."

"What was he doing with the money?" Agent Travis asked, concern lining his voice for her to hear.

"I asked him the same thing. He said he wanted to return it to collect a reward. Looking at him with a heavy load on each shoulder, I had my doubts about it. He had one broken hand, his gun in the other and me barely being able to walk. It seemed like more of a burden at that point. But there was no time to discuss it and we set off again down the trail, traveling slow and cautiously through the pines," Kate said.

"We had made it a good ways when we heard footsteps in the distance, someone was coming towards us. We froze and looked at each other before Jack began moving us off the trail again. There was a gully nearby and Jack helped me down into it. We stayed low and quiet. I was afraid to even breathe. Within a minute a man went running past us on the trail, back towards the cabin."

"Did you see the man who went by?" Agent Travis said.

"No, but Jack did and I can tell it made him nervous. He was already breathing heavy from carrying those bags. He inspected his broken hand and decided it was time to leave the money. He told me to stay down and to keep quiet as he hauled the money up the mountain. He rounded the corner and was temporarily out of my view but I could see he was headed for one of the ventilation shafts we had found in the Spring Hollow mine."

"It didn't take long for him to reappear without the money and breathing easier. He told me he had slid the money down the shaft, and would return for it later. He helped me back on my feet and back on the trail. From there we made good time back to the horses, even found poor Trigger waiting for us," she said, the smile returning to her face again.

"We mounted our horses and headed back the way we came through Birch Canyon so not to come across any more of their gang. I was glad to be going home, but when we got back, I knew we would have problems explaining all of this. We stayed out back, minding the horses, and talked about what we should say."

"Why not the truth?" Agent Travis asked curiously.

"Jack wanted to but it's not that simple," Kate said shaking her head.

"It sounds that simple," Travis countered.

"I wish it was, Agent Travis," Kate replied. "You don't know Logan. It's a nice place to live…if you fit in. But Jack was never accepted here, despite the fact that he was raised in Logan. He came from a broken home. He was quiet. He didn't look like one of us. It breaks my heart that he gets treated like an outsider. He reflects Cache Valley better than any two of us put together," Kate said, wrenching at the handkerchief in her lap.

"The fact is, if we told the truth, I might have never seen Jack again. If the authorities went up there and didn't find the gang, none of this Fast Eddie person, no trace of anything, how do you think that would look? The boy from the broken home with the drunk father and the beat up girlfriend," Kate said sternly. "Jack wouldn't stand a chance and I wasn't going to let that happen to him."

"So you made up the story about the accident in the cave," Agent Travis said.

"Yes, we did," Kate said. "I knew it wasn't great but it got us by, barely. It was a choice that had to be made."

"But choices have consequences," Travis noted.

"Yes, they do," Kate agreed, pressing her lips together.

Agent Travis set his notebook down and leaned back, staring aimlessly across the room. He had many thoughts circling in his mind. He needed to recover the money. He needed to find Jack. He needed to go after the bank robbers. And he would have to decide in which order. He rubbed his eyes, feeling mentally drained now by the long day, all while Kate sat patiently across from him.

Travis kept to his reclined position as he said, "Kate, I know this hasn't been easy for you, and I want to help you," watching her responses closely. "But there's something more I need to tell you. This Fast Eddie, the leader of the gang, he didn't die in that cabin. He's alive and he's been after Jack."

Travis watched Kate closely for any sign of a response. Other than the constant movement of her hands pulling at the fibers of a small white cloth, she didn't flinch. He decided it was time to up the ante.

"If you don't help me, it is quite possible you will never see Jack alive again."

16

Agent Travis' words cut into Kate with an indescribable agony. He had no idea the lengths she would go to help Jack. His words felt more like they were meant to punish her than be helpful. She also wondered if he was putting his own agenda ahead of what was best for the two them. She leaned forward in the chair to let her hair fall over her face as she tugged on the handkerchief, which had become her outlet from the strain. Will this nightmare ever end, she thought, as her eyes teared up.

She kept her head down for several minutes. When she was ready, she wiped her eyes and sat back slowly, now looking up at the ceiling as if she had a few choice words for God. But instead she chose to redirect her efforts and asked Agent Travis pointedly, "Do you think this is my fault?"

"Your fault?" Travis said surprised.

"Yes, did I do this to Jack?" she asked.

After taking time to give it a proper thought, Travis answered, "No, I don't think you did. From what I saw of Jack he is very capable of making his own choices."

"But maybe I caused it unknowingly…because of my father," she said hesitantly.

Travis furrowed his brow, unsure how that statement fit. "What does your father have to do with this?" he asked.

Kate's voice wavered. "He never approved of Jack. He has very high standards for his children. Someone like Jack is not who he pictured for his daughter. I'm sure of it, even if he's never told me directly. As I got older, he became more serious about keeping us apart. The last thing he wanted was for us to still be together when it came time to marry. I think he sensed early on that I was serious about Jack and he has been subtly working ever since to steer me away from him."

"Does Jack know?" Agent Travis said.

"He would have to have a very short memory not to," she said with a half-hearted laugh. I overheard them talking one evening, shortly after that day in the canyon. Jack had come over to see me." She turned to look out the front window. "My father was outside in the yard, working on the flowers, and stopped him as he came up the walk. I happened to be coming around the side of the house but I stopped when I saw them and listened in secret."

"What did he say?" Agent Travis said.

"He got up real close to Jack and told him that he knew we were lying. I think seeing me with bruises was the last straw for my father. I can still picture him with his finger in Jack's face. I've never seen my father that angry. He told Jack it took every ounce of strength he had not to return the beating to him right there on the spot. It was awful to hear."

"He continued on about how he would never allow Jack to marry me. I was paralyzed against that wall, listening to him decide my fate," Kate said sadly. "I love my father very much, Agent Travis, but I couldn't accept that. Jack was my world, my future. He still is," she said while wiping away another tear that had broken free.

"And let me guess, Jack didn't say a word back in his own defense, did he?" Agent Travis said with a saddening effect.

"Not a word. Not to my father. Not to me. He turned around and headed home," Kate said.

"I went over there the next day, determined to make sure he wasn't feeling alone, and forgotten. When I got there he was outside at work. I could tell he didn't seem like himself. I tried to cheer him up. It took some time but he eventually came around. We spent the rest of the day together. Still it was never quite the same after that. I began to feel like the others around here do, never really knowing Jack Pepper and what he's thinking. It breaks my heart to think about."

Kate closed her eyes. As she did, a tear escaped down the corner of one eye and raced down her cheek, only to be swallowed up in the handkerchief that Agent Travis had given her. She didn't like feeling vulnerable like this in front of a stranger but the pent up emotions had no more room to hide. It took a few minutes while Agent Travis waited patiently. Soon the emotional relief came and she continued.

"We had our good days though," she said, ready to move on to a brighter subject. "Days spent in the canyon, celebrating for no reason. Jack seemed to leave his cares behind once we got out of town. That's why I made up anniversaries and holidays for us," Kate said, smiling as she recollected. "I wish you could know the real Jack. He's strong, Agent Travis, in both heart and mind. You called it luck, but it's more than that."

"It's like the stories he tells about those early trappers that came to Cache Valley. They were clever and tough, able to overcome any difficulty. That's what made them into legends. Jack is like one of them. Now that he's back in Logan, he has the advantage. This is his home. I suspect that is one reason he came back. If he has to fight, he will want to do it here."

Agent Travis sat across from Kate with a contemplating look. She studied him while he studied her words. Travis picked up his notebook and began to skim over the pages, making sure nothing was missed this time, the rustling of the pages providing the only resistance to the silence that was settling in.

"I still don't think it is your fault," he said eventually. "Maybe returning the money and collecting a reward was one way of measuring up for Jack, to be accepted, but the blow up with your father happened later. From what you said, he was looking for a reason to send Jack packing already. With the made up story of the accident in the mine, you gave him the perfect motive," his full perceptive skills on display in his conclusion. He wasn't about to miss tying facts together correctly again, both the physical and mental. "Either way, it wasn't your doing. It would be best not to dwell on that further."

Agent Travis got up and stretched his back. The sun had gone down. He slowly wandered the room looking at the items on display. Kate could tell he was doing more thinking than looking. She wondered if she shouldn't keep talking but she didn't have any more energy for it. Her stomach still tight, she wanted to go up to her room and curl up in a ball on her bed until it passed.

"So that's it then?" Agent Travis asked. "Jack goes after the bad guys and I make sure you are safe? That's Jack's plan?"

"It would seem so, Agent Travis," Kate said.

"And you are going to sit and wait?" Travis said in a skeptical manner.

"It's what Jack would want me to do," she answered.

Agent Travis took another long look around before looking at his watch. "When's your father coming home?" he said.

"Soon," Kate said, realizing that her lies were about to be exposed. "You're not going to tell him, are you?" she asked as she rose suddenly from her chair.

"He is going to find out soon enough," Agent Travis said pausing. "But, that really should come from you, Ms. Austin. I have to be leaving anyway. I need to call home to let my wife know I will be staying in Logan tonight. Then come tomorrow, you're going to help me find Jack. There will be no discussion about that either. We find Jack, we get you both to a safe place and the FBI will take it from there. Understood?"

Knowing she didn't have the wherewithal to negotiate, she solemnly nodded her head. Kate offered Agent Travis his handkerchief back as he walked by her.

"Keep it," Agent Travis said, wrapping her hand around it. "And try not to worry. I am sure you are right. Jack struck me as a survivor too."

Agent Travis made his way to the door before offering a sincere "goodnight" and stepped out into the night. Kate closed the door behind him. She walked back to her spot at the window, parted the curtains and watched as he got into his car. The engine revved and he pulled the car into their driveway, before backing out and heading down the general slope of their street, towards town.

Kate's hand unconsciously fell and the curtain closed. She turned back to the room and stood still. She was emotionally exhausted. The idea to head upstairs to the comfort of her bed was still top of mind, but she quickly dismissed it. She made her way back to the sofa and sat down. In the past few hours, her world had been turned upside down. She didn't know whether to be happy or sad or afraid.

She lay back on the sofa, arms draped at her sides, staring at the ceiling. She felt her muscles relaxing. In deep contemplation she considered her next move. What would her father think, she thought, when he found out? Could she wait until tomorrow as Agent Travis had instructed her? When would Jack come to see her? She found it all overwhelming.

As the clock ticked and the questions spiraled their way through her mind, one question began to separate itself from the others. It was a question that needed no answer. And it was that question that brought Kate up. She said it out loud as she rose to her feet.

"How can I stay here, for even one more minute, when I know exactly where to find Jack?"

17

Kate pulled her hair back, securing it with a rubber band before splashing water on her face. The water was cold but she didn't have time to wait for it to heat up. She grabbed a towel and dabbed at her skin, looking at her reflection in the mirror. If she was going to talk to Billy tonight, she would need to look as normal as possible. She couldn't let him know something was wrong from her tear-swollen eyes. And she definitely wasn't going to tell him the reason she was calling it off was because Jack was back in town. No, that would have to wait for this mess to be straightened out first. Besides, as much as she respected Billy, he was no Jack. There simply wasn't time to worry about Billy's feelings while Jack was out there fighting for their lives.

Kate changed into a long sleeved shirt which she tucked into blue jeans, secured by a belt with a country-style silver buckle. She slid on her hiking boots. They were tan and made of leather that rose just above her ankles. As she reached down and tied the yellow laces, she felt more like herself. Even though most people knew her for manners and her intellect, that reflected the growing movement of independent women, she didn't see herself that way. While she was proud of her small accomplishments, if the truth be told, she would always be more at home as a country girl.

She checked the mirror and mumbled under her breath "that'll have to do" as she grabbed a sweater, hurried noisily down the stairs and rushed out the door, giving it an unintentional slam due to a sudden swell of energy.

Billy lived on the next street over but down a ways. It was a ten minute walk that her anxious feet would do in less time tonight. The temperature had cooled and fall was showing signs of setting in. It was the kind of night she would normally enjoy a leisurely walk but tonight her pace was brisk as she tried to keep her thoughts on what she would say to Billy. The effort proved to be in vain as they kept finding their way back to Jack. A few hours ago she didn't know if he was alive but soon she would be on her way to see him. It's a funny thing how fate finds a way, she thought.

As she turned the corner, she could see Billy's home in the distance. A short breeze blew over her and she followed it with her eyes as it rushed towards the canyon. It wouldn't be long until she was headed in the same direction.

The Hendricks' home was now directly in front of her. The lights coming through the windows served as a warning that it was time to focus. She apprehensively walked up the path to the door and knocked.

Immediately the door swung open and Billy appeared, as if expecting her. This caught Kate off-guard. "Billy, you startled me," she said, noticing that she was about out of breath from the energetic pace of her walk. "I wasn't expecting you to answer so soon."

"I wasn't expecting you either," he said with a smile. "But it is a nice surprise."

Kate noticed the jacket and keys in his hand and pointed to them as she asked, "Were you going somewhere?"

"Well, I am not a door man. I wasn't standing here waiting for someone to knock," he said jokingly.

Kate's forced laugh was an ill-fated attempt that she was sure wouldn't go unnoticed.

"But," Billy continued, "I am in no hurry. Why don't you come inside?"

Kate accepted and they stepped into the living room off the entry way. Billy turned on a light and took a seat next to her on the couch, sliding his hand into hers in the process.

She sighed. She knew this was going to be a hard conversation and any attempt by Billy for affection was only going to make it worse.

"You look like you have something on your mind," Billy said perceptively.

"Well yes, I do actually," Kate started. She looked at Billy and saw that he was waiting to hear what she had to say. He looked happy, something that was occurring often since she agreed to their first date. She knew that was about to change.

"Billy, I don't think we should see each other anymore," she said. She watched his smile slowly fade. "You've been really terrific but I'm just not ready. I need some time before I can start thinking about anyone in that way."

She expected to get an earful of reasons why they should continue dating given his previous persistence but instead he just sat there, the silence reigning. Realizing that they were holding hands still, Kate slowly pulled her hand away and Billy's eyes fell to watch them untangle. It was more uncomfortable then she could have imagined. The clock on the wall ticked eternally slow. She wondered if he was ever going to speak.

Soon enough a voice came bounding around the corner with a "there are the two lovebirds." It was Billy's mother. She looked happier than Billy had a moment ago as she grinned from ear-to-ear at her quip.

Kate turned to say hello and Mrs. Hendricks asked how she was, along with a few other pointless questions, before realizing she had interrupted something, her real smile turning fake as she eventually excused herself. Kate turned back to Billy to find him staring straight ahead at the coffee table with a disgruntled look on his face.

"Billy?" she said softly.

"Can you at least give me a reason why?" he asked, his head and eyes never moving.

Kate hung her head and answered honestly, "No, I can't."

With that Billy stood up and walked towards the door and opened it widely with no words. Kate took that as her cue to leave. She got up from the couch and made her way to the door, stopping to say, "I'm sorry." Billy pulled away his gaze from her in a defiant manner and said nothing. She stepped out the door which closed quickly behind her.

She walked away from the home eagerly; glad to be done with that unpleasant task. It's not how she had wanted it to go but there was little she could do for Billy now. She promised in her heart to smooth this over later but she wasn't sure it would matter. The look in Billy's eye gave her little hope that they would be friends again anytime soon.

Nevertheless, the deed was done and her thoughts turned enthusiastically to Jack. She practically ran home, entering the front door with a loud "hello" expecting her father to answer. Instead Trigger, came around the corner from the kitchen and looked at her. She ran to him and slid to her knees saying, "He's back Trigger. He's finally back!" as she scratched his ears vigorously. Trigger looked at her as if he understood and panted his approval.

"There's no time to waste," she said. "Let's go see him."

Recognizing that her father must have been held up at the meeting, she elected to leave a note. She kept it simple, saying she would be staying in her girlfriend's dorm room on-campus after a late night social event. It would please him to hear she was out socializing. She felt a tinge of guilt in lying to her father but justified it as necessary given the environment he had created by even the slightest mention of Jack.

She rushed up the stairs and then back down again with a half-filled backpack. She threw in a few more essentials before heading into the kitchen to fill a canteen with water. The trip wasn't far, nor dangerous under normal circumstances, but she wasn't a novice to the outdoors either. She knew she should go prepared, the thought making her smile as Jack had always been proud of her skills in the back country.

With that, she and Trigger headed out the back door, jumping off the porch and landing in stride, walking straight towards Green Canyon. If all went well, she would be with Jack in about an hour's time.

Billy entered the Bluebird restaurant haphazardly. He looked up only long enough to check the crowd. He didn't see anyone he recognized, which was exactly what he had hoped. He wanted to be left alone. While out on his errands, his thoughts had been cycling through what had turned Kate, not to mention the embarrassment he felt about his mother coming in mid-breakup. He wasn't ready to return home yet.

He moved his way to the bar and parked on the stool next to where he and Kate had sat on their first date only a few weeks back. He looked down to them as if they would provide some answers. They didn't.

"What can I get for you?" a girl behind the counter asked.

He looked up and shrugged, "Whatever."

She looked confused. "Are you hungry?" she asked.

Not in the mood to talk, he replied, "A pop is fine." That did the trick as she set off to get him one.

He sat still, looking down at the counter, the rage building slowly inside. He had waited a long time to have an opportunity with Kate. All those years he had taken a back seat to Jack and now that it was his chance, he got only a few dates, a few kisses and no good reasons for it to end. He knew Jack was gone. No one had heard a word from him, including Kate, but still he somehow assumed this was Jack's fault.

"Hey son," a man said from the table behind him.

Billy ignored it, too self-absorbed to care to find out if someone was talking to him.

"Son, I'm talking to you," came the raspy voice again.

Slowly, Billy slid around on his bar stool and raised his head. Four men sat at the table behind him, having just finished a meal. They all had their eyes fixed on him and their looks brought Billy to attention.

"I am looking for someone," the man continued. He was a large man, and ugly. He was picking out his teeth with a tooth pick between sentences with his other arm resting on his gut. "A young man, probably about your age. I am wondering if you can help me find him."

"Who is it?" Billy said curiously.

"His name is Jack. Jack Pepper."

Billy nearly fell off his seat, the previous questions plaguing his mind now answered.

"I went by his place," the man continued, "but it's been sold. I wanted to pay him a visit but no one's seen him around."

"He's been gone for a year or so," Billy replied. "No one knows where."

"Not no more," the man said gruffly. "He's come back. That I'm sure of. Seen him myself up in the canyon. But I can't seem to track him down. Do you have any idea where he might be staying?"

Billy looked at the other men again. They were hardened men that looked up to no good, and were obviously strangers to Logan. His better judgment told him it was best not to share any information. "Sorry, can't help you," he said finally as he turned back to the bar.

"Are you sure?" the voice said again. "You looked like you might know."

Billy kept his head down, staring at his drink, the bubbling soda in front of him offering little in terms of advice. His breakup with Kate was about Jack after all, he thought. He could feel his face getting hot. He had lost out to Jack once again. The image of Kate from earlier in the evening flashed through his mind, reminding him of the reason he was there in the first place. He had a sudden change of heart. He pushed off the bar to turn back to the men and said, “You know, there is this one place you could look.”

18

Kate entered the mouth of the canyon with Trigger nudging along at her side. She was sure he didn't mind a long walk. Trigger was always game for an adventure, and had been called on often as a substitute with Jack gone. She had made this trip so many times that Kate felt confident even at night. With a full moon to assist, she had more than enough light for the journey.

As she made the routine steps, she thought back to all the times she and Jack spent together on William Hendricks' land. The pasture had a barbwire fence that ran the length of it to keep in the cows. The only access by car was to keep going along the dirt road, past where the paved road ended about half way up Green Canyon. After another mile you would come to a locked gate that maintained the outer perimeter of the property.

The gate provided a barrier from the rest of the world. If it was open, they knew Mr. Hendricks (or one of his sons) was on site working. That didn't create any issues as they had already been given permission to be around given they left things as they were. They just made sure to steer clear of any work being done. If it was closed, Jack and Kate knew they would be safe and alone on the property. If anyone came by vehicle they would hear them coming before they would see them.

Given the choice between the two, they preferred to be alone. It gave them free reign to practice having a life together, unencumbered by the tensions others created for them. This is when it became their kingdom, almost like a dream, and on most days, it was perfect.

At night the gate was sure to be locked. She would crawl through the barbwire fence (a task that was far easier when Jack was there to hold the wires apart) and travel across the field to the wooded area on the other side. There nestled behind some trees up against the mountain was her destination. The Hendricks feed and supply barn.

When described for its purpose it didn't sound like much, but it was, in fact, quite special. It was built to look more like a log cabin. It's possible that was its original intended use. The structure had high side walls topped off by a bright red roof made of tin, the roof sloping sharply to alleviate the large annual snowfall that it would incur. The front door sat squarely in the center of the building with a window on each side. There was a small awning that covered the door, a few steps and the landing. The side walls were absent windows but one contained a large fireplace that jetted out the top of the roof. The dirt road leading up to it went around back where a more traditional barn double-door was concealed. When fully open, you could easily drive a pick-up truck inside to load or unload hay.

The front door was locked but the back door was simply secured with a latch. Mr. Hendricks had little need to secure that building. As long as the gate was locked, no one would be able to haul away the barn's contents, unless someone was willing to drag a bale of hay, or heavy equipment, several hundred yards to the fence. No, that kind of crime was unheard of in Logan. It was code amongst ranchers and farmers to leave other's livelihoods alone.

Kate loved being inside the Hendricks barn. It was like her home away from home. Depending on the season, it would be somewhere between full or empty with either grass or alfalfa hay. She loved the smell that filled the air as she associated it with the good times she and Jack had there. In the center of the room was a table where she and Jack would eat. They would sometimes start a fire in the fireplace to keep warm. But her favorite feature of all was the loft.

The loft extended about half the length of the building with a ladder as the only way up or down. Typically there was hay in the loft for longer-term storage as it kept better when off the ground. She and Jack had enjoyed many afternoons talking or napping together up there as they rested following their excursions. It was the time they would share their deepest thoughts and dreams. Jack could turn into a regular chatterbox when it came to talking about all the things he wanted to accomplish – a ranch of his own, a wife to care for, a large family and, of course, Trigger, were all part of the plan. It was in this time together that Kate knew they were made for each other.

No one knew about their time together in the barn, except for maybe Mr. Hendricks. He must have noticed the unintentional use it incurred. But he never said anything about it, and neither did she or Jack, for fear that someone would get the wrong idea about what they did there. Their time together there was private, but innocent, and there was no reason to let anyone think different.

Kate knew this is where Jack would be hiding. The cabin is virtually unseen from the road to the gate. You would have to cross into the property to even know it was there. A perfect hideout.

She was anxious to get there and increased her pace. She turned off the trail and crossed over the stream on a log Jack placed there several years ago. As far as she knew, she was now on a path that only she and Jack traveled. It was concealed by scrub oak and willows, thus making it darker in the night. Her heart beat a little faster and she whispered to Trigger, "over halfway there, don't be getting scared now just because of the dark." Despite her encouraging words, she was working harder now to stay calm, not knowing whether it was the lack of light or the news from Agent Travis that was stirring up the fear in her mind.

She stopped to retrieve a flashlight from the backpack. Her feet knew the steps, but her mind needed reassurance. She began again and had made it no more than ten steps when she heard something. She froze in her tracks. The sound came from behind her. She dropped to one knee and looked back, shutting the light off, and peering into the darkness, her eyes trying to adjust. Trigger stopped next to her.

"Shhh," she said in a whisper, advising herself as much as the dog.

What was that, she thought. It sounded like a rock rolling down the path. Unless rocks move on their own, there was someone back there that had caused it to move. Her mind turned for other conclusions; an animal, a rock falling from the mountain, the sound of the stream. Each was plausible but they would all require her to give up her naturally-drawn conclusion – someone had kicked a rock.

Get up Kate, she told herself. This is no time to be chicken. She forced herself up. If there was someone back there, the only way was forward anyway, and she knew Trigger would let her know if that someone got too close. She picked up the pace, just shy of running.

As she went, her memories of Jack and the barn ceased in order for her to put all of her mental energy into listening. She knew the sounds of the canyon. She knew how canyon sound was different from the valley, how things echoed and reverberated, how everything was magnified. She knew what she should hear and what she shouldn't, like rocks bouncing on the trail. If something was out of place, she would pick it up faster in the canyon. She used that to her advantage as she kept her head rotating and listening as she progressed down through the trees.

It had been fifteen minutes since she heard the sound when she had to stop for a break. Her lungs were burning and she needed water. She dropped to one knee again with an eye back towards the way she had come. She unscrewed the canteen lid as quietly as she could and took a drink. Trigger had sat down in front of her expecting a drink of his own. She poured some water in her cupped hand for him. He noisily lapped up the water before looking up for more.

"Oh Trigger, could you be any louder," Kate said softly. She would usually give him plenty of time to drink but she was antsy sitting in the middle of the woods. She would be an easy target if someone meant to do her harm. She hadn't heard another sound but she had a feeling she was being watched. She gave Trigger one more handful and put the canteen away. "You'll get more soon, I promise," she said as she leaned in to give him a kiss on the nose.

Kate could see she was almost to the opening in the trees that lead to the gate. She pushed on with a new determination not to come up short when she was so close. Her feet moved even faster as she neared the opening, the trees beginning to thin out around her, allowing more light from the moon. She turned her flashlight off now that she could see enough to gauge her footing. No need to give away my position, she thought.

Despite her tactical planning and being so close to her destination, her quickened pace seemed to bring greater angst. Even in nearly a full run, she half expected a hand to grab her from behind any moment. She pressed on, trying to out run the fear.

The field was dead ahead, glowing in the moon light. She felt a ray of hope. Once she cleared the trees it was a fifty yard dash to the fence and then a few hundred yards across the field to the barn. "Come on, Trigger," she said out loud, racing towards the light, her backpack swinging wildly on her shoulders as she anticipated the freedom the light would bring. Trigger ran ahead, breeching the tree line first, when Kate suddenly came to a screeching halt.

Trigger had gone forward several yards before stopping when he realized he was alone. She watched him look back as she held fast to the final tree. She looked back and saw nothing.

She wanted to run but doubt had begun to fill her mind. Out in the field she would be an easy target, nowhere to hide and if Jack wasn't there, she was all alone. No one knew where she was. There would be no help coming. Even if she could get to the building, she couldn't stop anyone from following her in. All her thoughts and fears combined against her as Trigger stood patiently in the field looking back at her.

She glanced back and then forward again, deciding what she should do. She remembered her ordeal in the mine and wondered if she should pray. It had worked once before but there had been many times since that she had left plenty of unanswered messages at God's door. She had doubts but she decided to leave one more.

She bowed her head and in a whisper, she said, "Father in heaven, if we make it through this ordeal, I will strive to live my life for Thee always, doing Thy will above my own. But if I don't make it, please let Jack be ok. He deserves it more than anyone I know. In Jesus' name, amen."

Kate opened her eyes before the final words left her lips, looking back to make sure no one was there. She was still scared but felt more assured about what to do. She took a deep breath, let go of the tree and stepped forward into the field, walking at a normal pace towards Trigger. Her heart was beating frantically. She was still breathing heavily but a smile emerged on her face as she came closer to her traveling companion.

She reached Trigger and stopped to kneel down and scratch behind his ears. "That wasn't so bad, was it boy?" she said as she glanced back. She didn't see anything and turned back to Trigger, who reached up and licked her face. She closed her eyes and mouth as his doggie breath covered her face. She pulled away and smiled back down to him, enjoying the moment together until suddenly the moment ended with the sound of a branch breaking behind her.

Trigger's head turned to look back, signifying he heard it too. She froze, this time not even bothering to look back. In a word, she gave instruction to Trigger, "Run boy!" and she bolted towards the fence, urging her legs faster than she ever had before. Trigger ran next to her, never leaving her side.

She could see the barbwire fence dead ahead. She could see the Hendricks land beyond that and, even with the horizon bouncing in front of her as she ran, she could barely make out the red roof of the barn at the opposite end of the valley.

As she ran, her mind sent one more message towards heaven above, "Please let Jack be there."

19

Jack lay comfortably asleep on an old blanket, the events of the past week leaving him exhausted. Sleep had fled on most nights and he was left to run circles in his mind, chasing thoughts and ideas to alleviate this current predicament. At times, he could no longer tell when he was awake or asleep. He was lost in between consciousness, but he found that to be his most productive time as he developed his plan. He could see things more clearly then. He played them out over and over, how he was going to beat Eddie.

The downside was it left him tired during the day. This afternoon however, sleep finally found him. As soon as he lost the men on the ridge, he returned to find the exhaustion had finally overcome him, and he slept.

He had spent the last several hours adrift in the dream world. He didn't often remember his dreams and even less often found meaning in them, but this night he did. Tonight he dreamed of his mother.

He could see her outside, in a field, smiling at him in the distance. She wore a summer's dress, an off-white color that extended from her wrists to her ankles. It was made of a light material that was blowing in the breeze. In his dream, he looked around. The day seemed unusually bright.

She looked a few years older, as his mind might imagine her. He called out to her and waved, but she only smiled back, apparently unable to speak to him. It didn't matter. The look on her face told him she was happy. He was smiling back at her, waving his hat above his head. It felt like to Jack the moment was free from the barriers of time. He didn't know how long they looked at each other but it didn't seem to matter. It wasn't uncomfortable and he didn't mind if it lasted hours. He relished the fact that he had finally found her.

Eventually, he sensed it was time to go and she turned to walk away. He called out one more time to her, and for some unknown reason, called her by name, "Alejandra." She didn't stop to look at him. He wanted to say goodbye and tried again. Still no response. He tried one more time, this time calling her "Mom."

She stopped and turned around, still smiling, her eyes a glow. "I'm sorry I left you, Jackie," she said. "I wish things had been different. I have missed you every day, more than you know."

Jack was speechless.

As she turned to leave, she paused and turned back with a final word of advice. "Remember Jackie, a man's strength lies within." His dream faded out as she walked away. He felt his whole body tingle with a warmth he couldn't describe.

Jack was awake now, even though he had yet to open his eyes. He elected to stay in the half conscious state, enjoying the sweetness of his dream. He was lying on his side and had one arm folded under his head as a pillow. Even with his eyes closed, he could tell it was night, further lessening any urgency to awake. He hoped maybe he could fall back asleep and see his mother again. As he waited, he felt relaxed, his body enjoying a warm, tingly sensation. It was for the first time in a long time he felt so at peace.

The longer he lay there, the more he realized his time to sleep was over. He rolled over and repositioned himself, arms now folded over his chest. Kate's face appeared in his mind. It wasn't there long enough to enjoy before he saw Billy's too. As much as he only wanted to think about Kate, he couldn't shake the memory of what he saw in her stable last week when he went to warn her.

It had been dark when he came down from the Hendricks property. He had hoped she would have retired to her room and he would be able to tap on the window to get her to come out. Instead, he saw a light in the stable as he approached. Wondering if it was her father, he approached with caution. He made his way up to the back of the stable and peaked through a crack in the boards. He had didn't have much of a view due to the structure's interior framing but he did hear her voice. Kate was in there, and she was laughing.

He made his way around the corner and along the side of the building towards the light, until he found a new crack to peer through. He could see her then. She looked happy. She was talking to someone outside of his limited view. Jack smiled at seeing her. She was just as pretty as ever.

He was about to head around to the front of the stable when he heard another voice. He listened, knowing it sounded familiar. The stranger spoke again and Jack immediately recognized it. It was Billy. Jack straightened up in disbelief and watched as Billy stepped into the light.

"I didn't know you loved horses so much," Billy said.

"Ever since I was a little girl," she replied. Jack could sense she was nervous.

"They are good companions, aren't they?" Billy said. "We should go riding together. Maybe up Green Canyon."

Kate looked down at the suggestion. "Maybe," she finally answered him.

Billy moved closer to her, but she stepped away pretending to look at a bridle hanging on a post.

Jack grew tense by what he saw. He was surprised to see how light and fluid the interaction between them was. He could tell this was more than two friends catching up on old times. His mind passed him a thought that maybe he should slip away but his heart was in control now and Jack wasn't going anywhere. He watched on.

"Well, maybe you will feel about me the way you do about these horses," Billy said, breaking the silence. Kate didn't answer. "Shoot, I would settle for half that much," he said jokingly to relieve the pressure of his last comment.

When Billy saw that Kate still hadn't responded, he decided to press the issue, "Because I already feel that way about you now, have for a long time as a matter of fact."

Kate couldn't hide from his comments any longer and said, "I know, Billy. I do. You are very special to me too," still not looking up at him.

"Then why don't you come a little closer?" Billy said confidently.

Kate hesitated but moved closer to him. When she was in his reach, he pulled her in close with a less than romantic jerk and put his arm around her waist. She had put both of her arms up in front of her chest to create some separation as they touched. Billy used his other hand to tilt her chin up to him. He brushed her hair back and took his time as he looked into her eyes. Kate didn't say a word.

Jack couldn't take his eyes off the two of them as he watched the train wreck that had become his life fall further into the ditch of despair. He knew it wasn't his right to have hoped that she would wait this long. He knew it was his decision to leave town. He knew she was free to choose whoever she wanted even if he had stayed. But despite all of this, he kept hoping Kate would change her mind and push Billy away. Don't do it, he willed to her in his mind.

But his thoughts didn't prevail. Billy dipped his head to kiss her lips. Jack dropped his head, unable to watch.

There were no more words coming from the stable as he looked down. No more clever talk from Billy. No more reluctant comments from Kate. He felt both sick and numb as he stood there.

Finally, his mind wrenched back control and he set to leave when he turned to notice a figure towards the front of the stable silently watching him. It was Trigger. Despite his immense personal pain, he smiled when he saw him. He was a sight for sore eyes. Jack took a knee and Trigger immediately walked over to him. Jack knew what was coming and put his head down so Trigger could shower him with kisses. Trying again to will his thoughts toward Kate, he thought, I like my kissing companion better than yours.

Jack kept quiet and so did Trigger as they enjoyed their reunion. In a vengeful moment, he thought about taking Trigger with him right then and there, but as much as he wanted his dog back, he knew Trigger could do more to protect Kate then he could. Despite what was happening on the other side of the wall, he decided he would see this through, no matter how much it hurt.

As he got up to leave, Trigger looked like he wanted to follow Jack but Jack's motions persuaded Trigger to stay put. Trigger circled a couple times with anxiety in watching Jack, letting out a whimper in the process. Jack could hear talking again from inside the stable. He picked up his pace as he moved further away from the Austin home.

It wasn't at all how he thought that encounter would play out and now, as he lay with his eyes closed, he couldn't think of Kate without reliving it. Jack hoped his semi-conscious state would dull the pain but it didn't, and he was entirely awake now. He shifted again trying to shake the memory free. He now felt cold and reached down to wrap the old wool blanket over him.

As he lay in silence, trying to get warm, he heard a sound in the distance. That brought Jack's eyes wide open. He could hear someone coming towards the barn. He instantly sat up and slid on his boots. With pistol in hand, he made his way down the ladder, cursing the architect that made this building with windows that only faced out to the front.

He heard the footsteps getting closer. They stopped along the side of the house. He could tell someone had come to rest against the side wall. He stood just on the other side of the wall, listening. After a few seconds, their feet began to move again, making their way to the back of the house. He walked with them step-for-step, his arm out in front, gun facing to the ceiling.

As the perpetrator rounded the corner and walked towards the back door, Jack brought the gun forward, stabilized by his other hand and took a shooting stance. Shoot to kill, he thought. You've got nowhere left to run. He cocked the hammer as he heard the latch lift and moved his finger over the trigger. It would all be over in a second.

Before the door opened, a familiar voice said, "quiet boy." That got Jack's attention just in time as the door opened and moon light flooded around Kate's silhouette as she stepped in. Jack removed his finger from the trigger and pointed the gun down, watching her from the shadows. Trigger followed her in and she immediately drew the door closed, latching it from the inside. She collapsed her head against her arm, which was resting on the door as she tried to catch her breath.

Jack might have been content to remain in the shadows for a minute to sort out his emotions but Trigger immediately gave him away as he jogged over and jumped his front legs up on to Jack's thighs, looking up with excitement. Kate wheeled around when she realized what Trigger was up to. She watched as Trigger got down, circled and jumped up on Jack again in the same manner.

"He missed you," Kate said, turning on her flashlight to give them some light.

Jack didn't answer right away, only put his gun away and knelt down to interact with Trigger, scratching him behind the ears, before saying, "Well, I'm glad that one of you did."

Kate didn't respond so Jack kept playing with Trigger. He had missed his dog immensely. They had shared so much of his life together that it made him feel whole to be with him again. Trigger was better than any therapy money could buy.

After a few moments, he looked up to see a somber look from Kate, her eyes filling with pain, and tears. Her lack of response to his comment told him that she already knew why he had said that.

Neither spoke as the reunion with Trigger began to wind down. Jack stood up. The silence was painfully awkward and he tried to change the subject.

"I take it Agent Travis came to see you," he said.

"Yes, he came by the house today. We talked for a long while. I was glad to hear you were back, but I wish you had been the one to tell me," she said, jabbing back at him.

"You've been busy. Didn't think you could fit me into your busy days…and evenings," he shot back coolly.

"Then you've been away too long if that is what you think," Kate responded immediately, not willing to back down.

While Jack was sparring with Kate on the outside, his emotions were fighting him on the inside. He had missed her more than he could find the words to say. If he were being honest with himself, all he really wanted to do was to hold her, but every time he tried to let go of the hurt, and allow himself to be happy, he saw her and Billy together in his mind. That thought built up the walls inside of him even higher and the conflict resumed.

"I have been away too long apparently," Jack said, walking away from her now.

She followed on his heels, "Jack, I can explain. Will you let me explain?" she said, grabbing a handful of his shirt to stop him.

He stopped but didn't turn around, only hung his head and stood in silence.

She let go of his shirt and smoothed it out as she often does, the feeling of her hand on the back of his shoulder melting away at his defenses.

"Jack, I want to talk about it but I have to tell you something first," she said.

He didn't move, waiting for her to speak.

"I think someone is out there. I heard things while coming up the canyon. I can't say for sure, but I don't think we are alone."

Jack turned around, all business now, and looked in her eyes. She was about to speak again until Jack put a finger to his lips while he listened intently. They made eye contact the entire time he listened, which only served to make him want her back more. Conflicted, he needed some space.

He walked to the front windows and looked outside. He didn't see or hear anything. Could Fast Eddie and the gang have followed her to the cabin, he thought? He would have to think fast if they were in danger. After a minute, he came back to Kate and stood very close as he whispered in her ear, "Did you see anyone?"

She shifted her face so it was right next to his, intentionally grazing up against him before whispering in his ear, "No, I only heard something, twice. It was coming from behind us as we made our way up the trail."

Her warm breath on his neck caused the hairs on the back of his neck to rise. It was like a kick through the walls he had built around his heart. He had trouble resisting. He put his hand on the back of her waist and pulled her slowly towards him. "Where exactly did you hear it?" he said.

Kate swallowed hard and raised her hand to rest it on his bicep, acting like she needed something to pull herself closer to answer. "Just past the little stream with the log and then again right before the clearing," she said, tilting her head against his now.

He needed to go out and look around, but instead he stood with her, trying to come up with another question so he could stay near her. He moved his hand slowly and gently up her back, pulling her in more closely as he did, his left hand resting lightly on her hip. She felt electric to the touch.

Kate had both hands now resting on his arms as the two of them stood together in the dark, letting a year's worth of pent up energy surge through them, whatever resistance Jack had been offering her now completely evaporated. He wanted to forget about whoever was outside in the cold. He wanted to stay inside and enjoy the warmth. He remembered how being with Kate was all that mattered.

But before their lips would touch, and end any hope of Jack getting a look around outside, he stepped away, knowing that the right move was to keep them safe first. He looked down at Kate who pleaded with her eyes for him to be safe.

He reassured her by saying, "I'm coming right back this time. I just want to take a little look around."

She nodded her acceptance and with that, Jack headed for the back door, drawing his gun as he walked, feeling like nothing could stop him.

He paused at the door to listen while he lifted the latch and then, without another word, disappeared out the door, the moon light flashing in and then fading out as he went.

20

Jack had been gone for almost an hour. Kate was concerned but not overly. If anything had happened, she likely would have heard it. She knew Jack was cautious and was likely concealed somewhere watching for any signs of movement. Still she wanted him back with her. They had been apart too long for only a five-minute reunion. She ached for a chance to explain, to clear the air. She knew that if he would hear her out, how there was never a spark between her and Billy, and how she only ever thought about him, that he would understand. It became even more apparent to her now that most of her actions over the past year were meant to serve as a diversion, to mask the pain she felt of Jack being gone.

The time was passing slowly. She and Trigger huddled together on the main floor on a bale of hay. Trigger had fallen asleep at her feet after the long hike. "Not as young as you once were, are you boy?" she told him, running her fingers through his hair as he lay there.

Kate was tired too from the long day. She could feel her eyelids getting heavy, the dark of the barn tempting her to join Trigger in sleep, but she fought the impulse. She wanted to be awake when Jack returned. But in the end, nature won out. With her head resting comfortably against the hay stack next to her, she slept.

It felt like only a few minutes had passed when the back door of the barn opened, Jack materializing in the room. She awoke to see him close and latch the door. He was moving without concern of the noise it generated. She took that as a good sign. As he walked over to her, she remained seated. Trigger lifted his head as Jack sat down and gave a master's acknowledgement before plopping his head back down to continue with his nap, content that all was well around him.

"Hey," Kate said, her voice sounding like she had been asleep for a while. She reached for her flashlight and turned it on to serve as a makeshift lantern.

"Hey," Jack echoed in return. He sat on the edge of Kate's hay bale and loosened the laces on his boots.

"What did you see out there?" Kate asked.

"Not much," he answered. "Moved around to a few different spots, waiting for someone to give away their position but I didn't see anyone. I was thorough too. If someone was out there, they must be gone now."

"Oh," Kate said with a mix of relief and confusion as she knew she heard something. "Should we go or do you think we are safe?"

"I think we are safe for tonight…at least what's left of it," Jack said.

"What time is it?" Kate said.

Jack pulled out his father's watch and looked at it. "Just past 2 am," he said, looking everywhere except at Kate.

Kate straightened up even more as she realized she had slept far more than just a few minutes, not that it mattered. She had planned to spend the night here but she was surprised at how long Jack had been out there. He must be cold. The temperature inside the cabin had dropped sharply since he left.

"Are you cold?" she said, starting to get up. "I can get the blanket."

"No, I'm fine," he said, putting his hand on her leg to stop her. He flinched as if second guessing the contact he had just initiated.

Kate looked at his hand on her leg and decided to seize the opportunity, grabbing his hand as she sat up and said, "Jack, I am sorry about earlier. I didn't come up here to start trouble. I just…well, I just had to see you."

Jack didn't respond and she couldn't wait anymore. She leaned over Trigger and wrapped her arms tightly around Jack's neck, sensing the sudden show of emotion caught him off guard. He hesitated in reciprocating but Kate didn't care. She had a tight hold on him and she wasn't letting go for anything. She noticed Trigger raise his head again to check out what was going on above him, before lowering it again, obviously disinterested in something he had seen a thousand times before.

After a few awkward moments, which did little to convince her to let go, she felt one of Jack's arm come up around her back, followed shortly by the other, his embrace growing tighter in the process.

With her arms firmly around his neck, she entertained the idea of beginning to explain the situation with Billy, but now it all seemed so irrelevant. Instead, she chose another course and whispered in his ear, "I love you, Jack."

A few seconds passed.

"Don't you mean, Billy," he said slowly as he let go.

Reeling from his words, she let him withdraw. She watched as he got up and walked a few steps away, his hands on his hips and back to her.

"Jack, that's not fair," she said in protest. "It wasn't like that."

Jack said nothing.

Kate got up and followed after him. She approached slowly and reached up to touch the back of his arm. He pulled it away.

She folded her arms, not impressed with what Jack was doing to her. He knew this would hurt her, but she knew he was hurting too. "How was I to know if you were ever coming back?" she said.

"Because I told you I would," he said, his back still turned to her.

Angry, she raised her voice, "Jack, you weren't here. You don't know. Whatever you went through, it was just as hard for me. Don't do this."

She watched as Jack took a deep breath as he looked up at the ceiling. She didn't want to fight any more. They rarely disagreed and when they did it was civil. This was totally foreign to her and she didn't know how to fix it.

Jack slowly turned to face her. To her surprise, she saw a tear spill from his eye and dash down his face, he turned away quickly, wiping it off on his sleeve. She had never seen him cry before. It took her back. As she processed the scene, she thought, why are we doing this to each other?

On an impulse she quickly came forward and plunged into his chest. She wrapped her arms around him again and he did the same.

He didn't say anything, just kept holding her tight. Kate wasn't sure what was going on in his head but she didn't care. Her heart was beating rapidly.

She felt Jack's head as he tilted it toward her ear and whispered softly as he said, "I love you too," in return.

It was enough. She knew the fight was over. Neither one of them seemed to have the stomach for it.

She leaned in, her lips finding his, melding together, the grandeur signifying it was more than just a kiss. It was a kiss that meant he was never leaving her again. It was a kiss that meant they would never kiss another person the way they would kiss each other. It was a kiss that healed their wounds. All in the dim light of the barn, while Trigger slept on a bale of hay.

Eventually, they moved upstairs to the loft and the blanket. They lay nestled in the hay together, dividing their time between kissing and talking, with the former monopolizing the majority of the time. As the night passed, they delved into more weighty topics.

"Does Agent Travis know about the money?" Jack asked.

"Yes," Kate said shyly. "I told him."

To her surprise, Jack responded positively. "Good, that's for the best."

Apparently that is what he had wanted her to do. She paused with a perplexed look while searching for the right way to say her next words.

"Jack, why don't we just give this Fast Eddie the money? It might make him go away. We have to try," she said resting her hand on his chest as a reassurance.

"It might," he acknowledged while taking her hand in his, "but I think that money is the only thing keeping us alive." Jack was now the one searching for the right words. "Eddie isn't the kind of man that lets you bargain with him. And if he does, he wouldn't think twice about double-crossing you. I have been through this every which way and I don't see any way out, except," Jack said trailing off.

"Except what?" Kate said, fearing the answer.

"Except for me taking him head on," Jack said, cleaning it up to protect her feelings as much as he could.

Kate's face collapsed. She dreaded those words even though deep down she knew they were coming. "No," she finally said, "It's too dangerous. There has to be another way. Let's talk to my father. He can help us."

Jack sat up abruptly, letting go of her hand, knowing her father was not about to help him. He placed his arms at the top of his knees and looked downward, shaking his head like he had already thought through that. "Kate, if there was another way, I would have already tried it. There's not.

I have to get rid of this guy once and for all. He's not going to stop until one, or both, of us are dead."

"Jack, he has a gang. They're criminals…bank robbers. How can you win?" Kate said, sitting now alongside of him.

"I don't have to beat the whole gang. I think I just have to beat him, finish him off this time. I think that just might be enough to send the rest of them on their way. But if not, I will see it through. I'm not leaving Logan again," he said defiantly.

Kate lay back down, staring at the ceiling, the light of dawn allowing her to see the underside of the tin roof above her. She wanted to protest Jack's plan but how could she? In the end, he was right. They had been through this conversation before. All roads lead forward to conflict. It was their only chance to have peace, and a life together. But if Jack wasn't going to back down, then at least she could help.

"Jack, what can I do?" she asked gently, knowing he would try to dissuade her.

He turned to look at her and then lay down at her side. "It would be easier for me if you weren't here. If I knew you were somewhere safe. That's why I sent Agent Travis to you," he replied.

"Jack, you're asking me to walk away and leave you to your fate. Do you know how hard that is for me to hear? Never mind the fact that I will be sitting alone somewhere, not knowing if something has happened to you," she said fervidly. "That just won't do. I'm not leaving you to face this alone."

She watched him as he looked her over, doing her best to ward off his response with a determined look. Wanting to put forward a stronger case, she said, "I know this canyon just as well as you, Jack. I can help. Let me help you," she said, leaning in for effect.

Finally, after a long sigh, he said something that caught her completely unprepared. "Would you like to live with me someday, in our own house, here in Logan?"

Her hand drew up to her mouth in a look of surprise. She could feel the smile forming on her lips, with a new light coming from her eyes. She looked over at him suspiciously to make sure he wasn't joking. "Jack, what did you just ask me?" she said.

He rolled towards her, leaning up on an elbow and said with a straight face that was uniquely Jack, "I wanted to know if you would marry me."

Kate rolled away, on to her back, and covered her face with her hands. She didn't need even a moment to know the answer but she did need a moment to gain her composure. She felt ready to explode with something that she could only describe as a mix between a laugh and a cry. It was a feeling of utter happiness.

As she rolled back towards Jack, she said, "Of course I will marry you, Jack Pepper. All you had to do was ask." Kate leaned in to kiss her new fiancé. She was perfectly happy.

There would be no more discussion of Eddie and his gang for the time being. There was no talking for a while either. In fact, other than the sounds of a couple lying blissfully together, in the loft of a barn, at the end of a canyon, in the top of the mountains, there would be no other sound for some time.

That is until sometime later when Trigger, who had begun to sniff around the barn, was standing with his paws up on the front window, looking out as the sun peaked over the mountains from the east, began to bark.

Kate and Jack both sat up instantly and looked at each other, the uncommon sound immediately signaled a concern between them. Kate knew Trigger now as well as Jack did. She knew Trigger would bark for only one reason, if he sensed danger. There could be no mistaking it. If Trigger was barking, it meant someone was coming.

PART III

21

Jack sprung into action, quick to the ladder, sliding down by the rails, and heading off to grab his boots. Kate wasn't far behind him as they hurried to the window to see what Trigger had spotted. The dirty window obscured the view. Jack swiped at the dust to get a better look. Once the pane had been cleared, it didn't take him long to recognize the three men crossing the field.

"Is it them?" Kate asked nervously.

"Yes," Jack said somberly. "It's them."

Jack watched as they walked on a straight line towards their front door. They were still over a hundred yards out. He could make out the man in the middle with the shotgun as Eddie. To his left was another man who Jack couldn't place from that distance, but towering above them on the right was Donovan. He wore a long-sleeved red shirt and walked with a stride and pace longer than the rest, reminding Jack of the legend of Paul Bunyan. It wasn't a reassuring thought, knowing he may soon have to face off with him.

Jack stepped away from the window and pulled out his gun, checking it for ammunition. He reached into his pack and pulled out a hand full of bullets, which scattered as he dropped them haphazardly across the table. He checked his gun to make sure it was fully loaded before grabbing another handful and shoving them into his pocket.

He looked around for anything else that would help, his eyes scanning high and low. The barn was limited in its offering and he could see nothing else. He looked down at his gun again. It was all he had.

The dire nature of the situation was setting in with Kate. "Can we run?" she said as she grabbed Jack's arm, desperate to keep Jack from the conflict.

"It's too late for me," Jack said. "But that's exactly what I need you to do," as he took her by the hand towards the back door. She followed reluctantly, pleading with Jack to come with her. When they reached the back door, she pulled away, forcing him to turn and face her.

"Jack, please!" she begged. "I can't go on again without you. Please, let's slip out the back door and try to get away."

Jack looked at her face. It was filled with pain and anguish. He had already begun to prepare himself mentally for the fight, but he eased back now, knowing she needed his full attention.

"Kate, you won't have to go on without me. Did you forget? I have a wedding date to make," he said calmly. "But in order for me to do that, I have to go out and contend with these men. What I need for you to do, is to find Agent Travis and bring him here. You can sneak out the back and make your way to the Wind Caves Trail, take it over the ridge into Logan Canyon and then catch a ride into town. You know the way to the trail, right?"

She shook her head. He could tell her anxiety hadn't lessened but his command of the situation had won out and he knew she would be willing to go if he gave her a purpose, knowing full well that whatever was going to happen would be long over by the time she returned with Agent Travis.

He reached for the door to open it, but as he did she dove into him, pressing her whole body tightly into his. The feeling it produced caused him to momentarily forget the urgency of the situation. She felt better than anything he experienced in his short life on earth. It would be a waste, he thought, if he couldn't be around to experience this feeling over and over again with her.

"Don't you dare leave me alone at the altar, Jack Pepper," she whispered. "I'll never forgive you for that."

"Start picking out your dress then," Jack said boldly, pulling away slightly so she could see the look of certainty in his eye. "Now go. Be fast and be silent."

"I love you," Kate said as she leaned in for one more kiss.

Jack nodded as she went to leave. He had nothing more to say about it. His only thoughts were on how to make those promises come true.

As she left, he latched the back door and headed to the front of the barn. He peered again out the window and watched the incoming men to make sure they didn't look in Kate's direction with the intent to pursue her. Fortunately, they stayed the course, which meant he had only about a minute before they would be at his door.

"Well boy," he said to Trigger, "I think we better keep you inside for this one." He looked down on Trigger whose eyes reflected Jack's anxiety. "Don't worry, I won't hold it against you. I know you're not afraid."

Jack stole a glance outside before he closed his eyes and took a deep breath as he continued. "I, on the other hand, have to go out there, for the both of us. Don't show any fear now. You beat him before and you are just gonna have to go out there and beat him again," he said in an impromptu pep talk.

Jack held his eyes closed, slowed his breathing and waited for his head to clear. He reminded himself what he was made of. He knew he had it in him to win. In fact, he gave himself no other options—he had to win. He let it build until he felt ready. When he opened his eyes, the steely look had returned.

The next words came confidently, "A man's strength lies within."

As he spurred his courage, his fear began to recede. Now ready, Jack opened the door to face Fast Eddie and the gang.

Jack closed the door to a whimper from Trigger who was obviously not happy to be left out of the contest. With his hat low on his head and hands resting on his belt, Jack stood on the small, wooden porch and waited. He could hear Trigger scratching at the window where he had taken up position.

Eddie was close now, walking with a purpose, staring at Jack as he came up. At about twenty paces, he and his two men stopped. Jack could see now that Jimmy was the third man. Jimmy hadn't said much in their prior meetings so he didn't know what kind of man he was, but simply going by size, he was the least imposing of the three.

Jack could hear Eddie wheezing from the long walk, his prior injuries still plaguing him. Not interested in starting the conversation, Jack waited, the time for words long past. Eddie, however, never knew a time he didn't like to hear himself talk and started right in.

"Well kid, you've had a lot of what I call dumb luck," Eddie said emphatically. "Too bad for you that luck just ran out." He took a step forward and laid his shotgun across his arms. "I'll be having my money now."

Jack ignored the request. The money was the last thing on his mind. Instead he took a step forward. Eddie immediately swung his shotgun in Jack's direction. Jack ignored that too and walked slowly towards it. But his eyes weren't on Eddie. They were on Donovan.

As he closed the distance towards Eddie, he altered his course slightly until he came face-to-face with Donovan, or more accurately, face-to-shoulder. He stopped with just inches between them and looked up. Jack spoke first.

"He says I've been lucky. It seems to me the last time I saw you, the only thing separating you from me was a set of bars. But that was your luck, not mine," his eyes locked into Donovan's as he made his veiled threat.

Donovan had a confused, angry look on his face, knowing that he had just been insulted but not fully connecting the dots on what Jack had just said. It wasn't often someone dared directly insult him.

Eddie let out one of his obnoxious wheezing laughs and said to Donovan, "You want me to let you kill him, don't you?"

Jack mirrored Donovan as they turned to face Eddie, and at the same time, both men said, "Yeah."

Donovan turned back to Jack with a look of surprise. Jack's gaze stayed locked in step with Donovan's, not giving away any emotion of his own. He was looking for an advantage. He had already calculated that it was in his best interest to take out the strongest man first, but physical strength alone wouldn't be enough. He had to get under his skin, agitate him a bit, to increase the likelihood he would make a mistake when the time came.

"Well, not until I get my money," Eddie replied, while trying to decide what Jack was up to. His shotgun eased in his arms.

"I'll take you to your money," Jack replied. "But not until he apologizes."

"What for?" Eddie replied, sounding more interested than anything.

"Killing my father," Jack said boldly, eyes still locked in an icy glare at Donovan, neither man had yet to step back.

Out of the corner of his eyes, he could see Eddie drop his head, and the barrel of his gun, as he contemplated the situation. Jack had made a calculated guess that appeared to work. Donovan's lips curved up to form a mischievous smile, acknowledging the truth, that he was likely the one to have dealt Tom the deadly blow.

Eddie paused to shake his head at Jimmy, who smiled enthusiastically at the unfolding drama, before he turned back to the two of them.

"Well hell. Donovan, are you going to apologize to Jack?" he said in a sarcastic manner. Jimmy laughed out loud at the idea.

Donovan looked over at Eddie and laughed as well, although in a more apprehensive manner as the complexity of the situation continued to elude him. "No," he finally said directly into Jack's face, trying to regain some of his edge. His head nearly collided with Jack's but still Jack didn't move.

"Sorry Jack, Donovan doesn't want to apologize. I guess you'll have to wait until he's in a better mood," Eddie said, enjoying the negotiations.

"Or maybe I could beat it out of him?" Jack said defiantly, his eyes no longer leaving his opponent as an altercation was imminent.

That brought another roar of laughter from Jimmy and Eddie. Eddie nearly doubled over from that comment. Donovan's face grew red as he reached out and grabbed Jack by the shirt, practically lifting him off the ground.

"Wait, wait," Eddie shouted with a hand up, trying to catch his breath. He stood back to full height again.

"Well this I just got to see, but don't beat him too badly, Donovan. I need him to be able to walk. Remember, he's got to take us to our money," Eddie said. "Now both of you take off your guns and throw them off to the side. I want to be able to enjoy this."

Donovan shoved Jack backwards and eagerly reached down to begin taking off his holster. Jack continued the momentum Donovan's shove had given him and walked back towards the house, heading to the porch. He glanced at Trigger whose paw prints were covering the lower part of the window. He seemed ready and waiting for a command from Jack. Jack gave him a confident nod as he unlatched his gun belt and dropped it to the ground. Although nervous about not having his gun on him, he felt sure Eddie wouldn't kill him without first getting his money.

Jack turned to see that Donovan was an even distance between Fast Eddie and the Hendricks barn. He already had his hands up, balled into fists, anticipating the coming action. Jack strolled slowly to a spot opposite him and looked up at the sun, careful to let as much time pass as possible while Donovan grew antsy. As he rolled up both sleeves, Donovan began inching closer.

Eddie could see Jack delaying and spoke out, "I'll call him off if you've had a change of heart, boy."

Donovan reacted negatively to that suggestion as he looked over at Eddie and said, "No, it's too late for that. I want him…"

While Donovan was complaining, Jack hit him with an open handed strike directly to his throat, shoving his Adam's apple back into his wind pipe, rendering him unable to speak. Eddie and Jimmy were also speechless.

Donovan stumbled back, grabbing at his throat while he choked for air, but he didn't have much time to recover. Jack was the one in a full combat stance now, looking to strike again. Despite his surprise (and lack of air), Donovan regrouped and lunged at Jack.

The fight was on.

22

Jack leapt straight up in the air, completely clearing Donovan as he came in low. Donovan fell to the ground, dust flying up all around him. Jack circled behind him as Donovan rolled over to look at him. This was Jack's second chance to pounce while Donovan wasn't expecting it, but he decided instead it was best to wear him out versus getting caught in his grasp too early, allowing Donovan to use his size advantage. Jack stayed back while Donovan got up slowly, swiping at the dirt in frustration as he did.

"You like to fight dirty, don't you?" Donovan said.

"You're the one in the dirt," Jack quipped back, holding his stance and considering his next move.

Once on his feet, the two danced around, fists up and ready to let them fly. Donovan threw an occasional punch but Jack ducked or dodged, not unlike he had with Billy many years before. He was intent on using his speed as a weapon.

Donovan was breathing heavy already. Most fights with him probably didn't make it to a second round and Jack knew this. He was waiting to see Donovan's hands begin to drop and his breathing become more pronounced before he would strike again.

Eddie and Jimmy were off to the side yelling advice and encouraging the action. Trigger was barking loudly from inside the barn. All this commotion only served to spur on Donovan more, who was now becoming visibly frustrated that he couldn't land a punch on his nimble opponent.

As Jack circled again, he turned Donovan so that his gaze was looking up into the morning sun before letting loose on a spinning back kick, driving with all his might into Donovan's mid-section before quickly backing away. It caught Donovan dead center under the ribs, knocking the wind right out of him, his hands falling down to his sides. He gasped hard for air but none was able to enter or leave his lungs. He tried again and again to get air into his lungs but couldn't. He looked over at Eddie with a look of surprise, and embarrassment.

Jack seized the opportunity and stepped closer to Donovan, angling to get to the side of him. Donovan tried to circle away but Jack was too quick. He had his hands up under Donovan's right arm, pushing him with his full force and Donovan stumbled sideways. Jack kept his knees driving forward, avoiding Donovan's grasp, until Donovan's feet couldn't move sideways quick enough and down he went again. This time Jack purposefully went down with him.

Donovan landed hard on his side with Jack on top of him. In an instant, Jack had turned him and sat down on his chest, his knees pinning Donovan's arms to the ground. Donovan choked out a terrible scream with what little air he could muster. His biceps were being pinched into the bone and the pain was obviously more than he could bear. He was bucking hard to get Jack off of him, but Jack kept his weight centered and held the position, beginning to unload hard right hands to Donovan's face in the process.

The fight had moved them about twenty yards from the house but Jack could hear Trigger bouncing hard against the front door, barking frantically now. As Jack wailed away on Donovan, the front door to the barn suddenly popped open.

Jack looked back. Out came Trigger, running hard to Jack's aid. That sparked an immediate concern. Jack momentarily suspended the beating to look in Eddie's direction. Sure enough, Eddie had lowered his shotgun, following Trigger as he advanced towards the fight.

"No Trigger!" Jack yelled, but it was too late.

Bang! The gun went off. Trigger was knocked off his feet and rolled awkwardly for several feet before coming to rest. There were no signs of movement.

"Perfect shot," Eddie said, pumping out the shell as he spoke.

Jack was stunned. He wanted to scream, but the words never came. He thought about making a run for his gun.

Before he could, Donovan had managed to free an arm, grabbed Jack by the shirt and threw him off to the side. Donovan got to his feet, his face bloody, eyes enraged, and stumbled after Jack.

Jack scattered away, barely getting to his feet before Donovan could catch him, his head swimming from what Eddie had just done. He moved around like he had before but his eyes were on his dog more than Donovan. He wanted to go check on Trigger, but he knew that wouldn't happen. He had to refocus. Donovan continued to bear down on him, with Jack barely remaining out of his grasp.

Jack's anger was building inside as he watched Eddie and Jimmy continue in their amusement of the situation. He no longer cared about fighting Donovan. He wanted to have it out with Eddie right then and there. It was time to send that fat man to the grave and shut him up for good. But he knew in order for that to happen he had to finish Donovan first.

With his emotion taking over, Jack changed his strategy. He stepped towards Donovan, ducking underneath each time one of Donovan's fists passed by. He was now toe-to-toe with his larger opponent.

Fortunately, the added adrenaline served him well. He felt fast and precise as he relentlessly landed punch after punch to all areas of Donovan's face and mid-section. Donovan's hands were now down and down for good as Jack's superior strategy won out against his opponent's superior size. Donovan began to sway as combination punches came from all directions.

Jack was grunting with each strike. All the anger he had felt from Trigger to St. George to Kate's father accumulating behind each blow, adding meaning to the savage beating he was planting firmly on his adversary. He had made up his mind. He wasn't going to stop until Donovan went down. Eddie and Jimmy were no longer laughing.

With each shot, Jack thought it might be the last. He could tell Donovan was standing based on pure grit alone, not wanting to know what it was like to collapse in defeat. But before Jack could finish him, another shot rang out, signaling an end to the fight. Jack whirled around to see who it was. Eddie and Jimmy also turned. Coming out of the trees was Will, and with him, Kate.

The missing gang member was not so far off after all. He must have been sent into the trees ahead of time to prevent Jack from escaping out the back. The gang hadn't known Kate was with him, but the look in Eddie's eyes told Jack she was a welcome guest. Jack's heart sank in despair.

"That's enough you two," Eddie said, taking a few steps towards Will, to confirm what his eyes were showing him.

Kate walked side-by-side with Will, his hand held tight to her upper arm to make sure she didn't run. Her head was down, her walk despondent. Jack could only imagine what she was thinking, being marched back in front of Eddie.

Eddie waited until she was right in front of him until he spoke, putting his hand lightly on her face, "Well I'll be. I am guessing you wanted me to finish what we started back in the hideout, that's why you came back? I don't blame you. I will do you up right this time."

Jack watched as Kate looked up, anger and tears welling up in her eyes. She swatted away Eddie's hand. "You coward," she said with a humiliated look.

Jimmy bellowed loudly at her audacity. Eddie gave him a smug look before turning back to Kate, grabbing her harshly by the neck. "You feel this?" he said hoarsely as she struggled to breathe. "This is the gentlest I'm going to be with you once I get started."

Jack took a step forward to rush at Eddie, but his progress came to a swift halt by a large hand clamping down on his shoulder from behind. It was followed by a stiff elbow to the back of his head. Jack began to drop from the blow, but Donovan grabbed onto Jack's other arm to hold him up. Even in his weakened state, Donovan's grip was still strong. It was useless to struggle.

"You two keep an eye on this one," Eddie said to Will and Jimmy as he headed in Jack's direction.

Jack stood still as Eddie approached, the reality of their situation setting in through the groggy feeling. He had no more options. No more one-liners, no more quick strikes. He glanced in Trigger's direction. There were still no signs of movement. Jack hoped to see any signs of breathing. He couldn't see any. He knew then that Trigger was dead. He also knew he would likely be following him to the grave.

Jack's head hung low. He saw Eddie's boots invade his view of the ground below. He felt the cold barrel of the shotgun press up under his chin, raising his head, forced to look evil in the eye.

"I'm done playing," Eddie said tenaciously. "I'll give you one breath to tell me where my money is and then I blow your head into a thousand pieces, right here in front of your girl."

Jack struggled to find the words, any words, that would delay the inevitable, but he couldn't think clearly, and part of his mind waited only for the click of the gun that would send him to meet his Maker. His lips parted to speak, but the sound that came wasn't his. It was from Kate.

"I know where the money is," she yelled, louder than necessary to make sure she was heard in time.

Jack, Eddie, and Donovan all turned to look.

"I know where he hid it. I will take you to it. I will take you to it right now," she pleaded forcefully. "But only if you promise not to harm Jack."

Eddie turned to look at Jack, somewhat surprised by the offer. He leaned in, getting close enough that Jack could smell his rotten breath, and said quietly enough that only the three of them could hear, "Sounds like your dumb luck hasn't run out after all, at least not yet." He glanced up at Donovan with a smile. Donovan's bloody face produced a faint smile of his own, knowing Eddie wasn't going to live up to any deal he was about to make.

"I accept," Eddie barked back towards Kate, as he pulled back his shotgun from Jack's chin and headed off in Kate's direction, Jack's head falling back to its previous position.

Jack could hear as Kate reassured Eddie that she knew where the money is. Eddie, conversely reassured Kate that he wouldn't harm Jack. Once the deal was set, Eddie came walking back over to Jack once again.

Donovan was still holding Jack up by the arms when Eddie arrived. He lifted Jack's head by his hair before saying, "This one ain't in any shape to make the journey. Leave him here. Donovan, you stay behind and guard him. We'll come back once I've got the cash."

Jack watched as Eddie gave Donovan a look before dropping Jack's head again. Jack didn't know exactly what it meant but he was sure it wasn't good. Eddie headed back towards Kate again with an extra bounce to his step, obviously eager to finally have his money.

Jack looked over at Kate, the mental anguish hurting more than the physical pain. He couldn't stand to think of her heading off with that man.

She was staring back at him, like she wanted to say something. Jack thought she looked somewhat calm, at that moment, given the situation. He also had something to tell her. His lips parted and he mouthed the words, "I love you" to her. She nodded back, in almost the same manner he had when she said that to him just a short time ago.

"So where are we headed?" Eddie asked, effectively putting an end to their moment together.

Kate held her stare on Jack while she answered, "Spring Hollow mine."

23

Eddie stepped aside to have words with Will and Jimmy. While he did, Kate noticed Trigger's lifeless body on the ground. She had heard a gunshot but she hadn't realized until now what it was for. She put her hand over her mouth and fought back the tears. Trigger's death was her first realization that she might not live through the day.

She looked over to Jack, his stance uneven like he wasn't currently able to stand on his own. His head was down and Donovan continued to hold him upright, occasionally letting one arm go as he reached up to wipe the blood off his own face. Donovan wasn't looking so stable himself.

"Time to go. Lead the way, Doll," Fast Eddie said as he pointed his shotgun in her direction.

Kate turned to see Eddie standing close, his face radiating its villainous sneer. "This way," she said, as she turned back towards the trees.

Eddie instructed Will to walk in front so she couldn't run away. Kate was next, followed by Eddie. Jimmy took up the rear, all walking in a single file line. As they approached the tree line, Kate paused and put her hand on an Aspen tree, looking back to take one last look at the scene around the old Hendricks barn, her make-believe paradise now dashed to ruin.

"Ain't got time for sentimental goodbyes," Eddie said as he stepped into her view and motioned her forward with his gun.

She started forward again despondently, the sound of leaves being crushed like dreams under her feet.

"How far is it?" Eddie asked impatiently.

"Not far, less than a mile," she replied.

"It better not be far. I don't need any more of these nature walks. Your boyfriend didn't do me no favors when he shot me. Walking long distances ain't my strong suit no more," Eddie said.

Kate didn't respond. She just kept walking. She could feel Eddie close behind her and he wasn't about let her walk in peace. He leaned in towards her ear and whispered, "I bet you were surprised to see me again, weren't ya?" his hot breath landing on her skin. She felt contaminated by it, but she didn't want him to know how much it bothered her so she did her best to ignore it.

Eddie continued now in a louder voice for Jimmy and Will to hear. "You thought you could leave me for dead and walk away with my money. Thought you could outsmart Fast Eddie. Well you thought wrong," Eddie said arrogantly. "You're gonna have to try a lot harder than that."

This brought a laugh from Jimmy and Will, the three of them engaging in a back-and-forth banter of how smart they were. Kate was glad his attention turned to boasting as it took her out of his focus. She plodded along, thinking only of Jack, wondering if she would ever see him again. She started to contemplate her own fate with Eddie, and the nightmare that awaited her, but her mind pushed that away, choosing to think only about better days with Jack. He would still be her ray of hope, even if it was no longer realistic for him to save her. She needed something to hold on to.

As they got closer to the mine, she remembered the last time she had been inside. It was the day she and Jack had decided to play hide-and-seek. That was several years ago now. She wondered if she could remember her way around. The mine was complex, more than any other she had been in. This expedition also meant she would have to face her other great fear, the cold dark of being underground. She got the shivers just thinking about it.

"Hold up," Eddie said after they had walked for a while. "I need to catch my breath." Everyone came to a stop. Eddie walked off the trail and put his forearm against a tree as he struggled to breathe, the wheezing of his voice demonstrating how unfit he really was. Kate wondered how well he would do on the journey through Spring Hollow.

Eddie spoke once his breathing returned to a more normal wheeze.

"How long do you think your boyfriend is going to last with old Donovan looking after him?" an eerie smile dawning on his face.

"I assume that since you promised you wouldn't harm him that he will be just fine," Kate answered, trying to sound confident despite what he was hinting at.

"Oh, I did, I did," Eddie said, trying to act sincere. He scratched at the stubble on his face like he was searching his thoughts. "Of course," he said leaning towards Jimmy, "I don't recall Donovan saying he wouldn't harm Jack. Do you recall that Jimmy?" as the smile returned to his face.

Jimmy laughed before getting all serious and saying, "Now that you mention it, I sure don't recollect that either."

Kate stood resolutely, arms folded across her chest, her face getting hot in the process. Jack was right. Eddie had no intentions of keeping his word. She felt naïve for thinking he might.

Eddie saw her disapproval. He came closer and gave her a slow look up and down. Kate felt exposed. She shifted under his scrutiny, keeping her arms locked defiantly against her. She kept her eyes fixed on a random spot in the trees, trying not to show any weakness.

"I promise you this much. If your boy is dead when we get back, I promise it will have been quick. Donovan doesn't drag this sort of thing out. He's merciless."

Kate turned to look at him as she spoke, ready to give him a piece of her mind, "Your promises don't mean anything to me. You're nothing but a thief and a killer. It doesn't matter that you didn't pull the trigger. You'll still have Jack's death on your head," her usually polished demeanor giving way to her emotions.

Kate watched as Eddie contemplated what she said, knowing deep down he didn't care a lick about any moral consequences. She took a deep breath and continued, "But I'm not so sure your Donovan won't be the one who is dead by the time we get back. I saw the beating Jack must have given him. Surely, you remember Jack will do whatever is necessary," as she glanced down to the scar on Fast Eddie's neck.

Eddie looked annoyed now. Kate braced for his reaction, whether verbal or physical. She watched him wrestle with his anger before he cooled and walked away, saying "Well, there is one way we will know who won, isn't there boys?"

"You got that straight," Jimmy said while Will nodded.

Kate was confused. They were obviously alluding to something unknown to her. She didn't care to carry on any more conversation with these men then she absolutely had to, but with her curiosity peaked, she asked, "How's that?"

Eddie stopped and turned to answer her question, lifting two fingers as he did. "Two shots," he said.

"Two shots?" she asked. "What does that mean?"

"Around here we always fire two shots," Eddie answered, turning back to his men. "One for the kill," he said.

"And one for the fun of it!" the three of them rowdily answered in unison.

Kate looked away and shook her head. "You're animals. All of you," she said, beyond frustration.

Eddie ignored her while he crowed with his crew. Kate felt the sudden need for rest. She had been through an exhausting day and night, and it was catching up to her. She walked over to a rock and sat down, putting her head in her hands. How much longer must I endure this, she thought.

After what felt like only a few seconds, Eddie was ordering her up again. "How much farther we got to go?" he asked.

Kate got up slowly. She wiped the tears off her hands on to her pants and looked down the trail. "The entrance to the mine is only a little ways from here," she said while pointing. "A few more turns is all."

"That's good. Let's get moving then," Eddie said. Everyone fell back in line in their original formation. Kate noticed even Jimmy and Will knew it was best to do what Eddie said as they jumped to their positions, ready to head off for the final leg of the trek.

The remainder of the trip was as short as Kate said it would be. The mine had a road running right through the trees that stopped directly in front of the entrance. The entrance was about the size of a double-door opening. It was framed with railroad ties and had rail tracks that ended just outside the opening. There was an accordion style iron fence that pulled from one side to the other and was secured by a lock. The lock was old and rusted and no longer closed. It simply hung on the latch to keep the gate in place.

Eddie looked around, cautiously checking the surroundings. The mine entrance was relatively concealed. There were trees and boulders on both sides, impairing the view of anyone who might approach. Kate could see that he was uneasy with this set-up.

"Will, Jimmy. You two stay here and keep watch. Make sure no one sneaks up on us. If you see anyone at all then, Jimmy, I want you to come inside and holler so I know. But then stay out here. I need you two to keep the path clear for the getaway. Think of it like a bank. We don't want to get trapped inside," Eddie said adamantly. He was all business now.

Both men grunted and nodded that they understood as they took up positions on either side of the entrance, getting comfortable for the watch.

Eddie turned to Kate, staring her up and down once again before he said, "After you, Doll."

Kate felt another cold shiver shoot down her arm.

Just as they were about to head inside, a shot rang out in the distance. It froze them in their tracks. "Well, well," Eddie said, "it sounds like we have some action happening back at the barn."

Kate's heart skipped a beat. As much as she didn't want to admit it, the sound had come from the way they came. None of them could have known what it meant, but her imagination skipped forward to the worst possible outcome. She wanted to believe it was something other than that, but she was scared. She held her breath, as if that would help, praying for that to be the only shot they heard.

The four of them stood still, waiting. As Kate held her breath, she counted in her head. 1, 2, 3. She didn't know why she was counting. She just did it, like counting for the thunder after lightning. 9, 10, 11. Eddie stood patiently, also waiting for the confirmation, his face showing he wasn't sold on the outcome just yet. 16, 17, 18. Maybe if she could get to thirty before another shot was fired it would mean he was ok. 23, 24, 25. She was getting close. She was going to make it. 27, 28, 29.

Just as she went to think the number 30, a second shot rang out, the sound echoing through the canyon and piercing her through the heart – a direct hit. She turned towards the mine entrance, her ray of hope completely snuffed out. As she stared into the mine, she could feel the cold dark coming to out greet her.

24

A kick to the back of his knees from Donovan brought Jack to the ground. He remained there as Donovan walked over to pick up his firearm. Jack looked over to see Donovan fastening his gun belt. It was not a welcome sight. He looked back down at the dirt, struggling to regain his senses. The earth felt like it was moving underneath him, like he was floating on a raft in the ocean, and the spots in his vision remained. He would need more time to recover and was content to stay down. As he stared at the ground, he kept blinking, watching the spots disappear and reappear over and over.

Donovan stood not far off, feeling his face with his fingers, trying to determine the damage. Jack could see blood trickling down from his nose and a cut on his left cheek. His left eye had swollen nearly shut, and his lip was ballooning. After giving up trying to tell how bad the wounds were by touch, he walked over to the barn to see his reflection in the window. Jack could hear him murmuring at what he saw.

Donovan turned to spit blood in Jack's direction. "Boy, you're lucky I don't up and kill you right now," he said.

Jack didn't respond. He kept his eyes on the ground, blinking some more. He had never been hit on the head before, let alone by someone of Donovan's size, and was surprised at how long it was taking for the concussed feeling to leave. But despite the delay, he could tell with each passing minute there was improvement and he was beginning to think more clearly. And as he did, he realized the grave predicament he was in. Whatever was about to happen, would happen fast.

Donovan came back over to where Jack was kneeling. Jack looked up at him, the sun shining over Donovan's shoulder, adding to his stature. Donovan scowled and said, "Don't get me wrong, I am going to kill you, but not until your friend is out of ear shot. We don't want to cause a panic."

Jack remained silent. The news came as no surprise. He had figured as much even in his current state.

When Jack didn't reply, Donovan shrugged and stepped away again. The excitement was over. There would be no more direct contact.

As Jack leaned back to sit upright, he thought about how he had ended up in this situation. It didn't seem to matter how hard he tried, he was constantly being met with obstacles and coming up short. His attempts to deal with them through sacrifice and patience, never leaving the path that would take him back to Kate, had failed. It hurt Jack more than Donovan's elbow to know that they would lose out on living their dream. Despite this realization, it was somehow worth all the pain and mental anguish. The costs may be high when you fall in love, but he was willing to pay them.

Donovan left Jack on the ground for several more minutes before deciding it was now time. He stood across from him, a good ten yards away, and ordered him to get up. Jack looked up to see Donovan with his pistol out. This was to be Jack's last stand. The trees lined up behind both of them, the only witnesses to an execution, as the sun lighted the narrow strip of the Hendricks land.

As he attempted to stand, he was surprised to find his legs working better than expected. He had a better sense of gravity too, his equilibrium returning. He looked around and blinked. The spots were still there but they were smaller and there were fewer of them.

He looked over the scene slowly in each direction, calculating his chances. He didn't have much time, and even less resources, but he had to come up with something. He figured his only chance was to make a run for it. Regardless of which way he went, whether to the barn on his right or to the trees behind him, Donovan was sure to get off four or five rounds before he made it to cover. He guessed it unlikely Donovan would miss on all shots so he prepared himself mentally to keep running even if he was hit.

In the end he decided the best route was into the trees. Each step in that direction would move him away from Donovan, therefore increasing the probability the bullets would miss. If he altered his direction just slightly while he ran that may be enough to avoid a majority of the bullets. Once in the trees, he would make like the Northern Utah deer and bob and weave his way between them. If he made it deep enough into the forest, he could turn it into a game of cat and mouse, hopefully with him being the cat.

Jack wasn't overly optimistic about his plan, but it was the best he could do given the situation. Jack steadied himself as he focused his attention ahead. He tried to look fatigued so he could catch Donovan off guard when he decided to bolt. A breeze ruffled the leaves and sent a few spinning to the ground, their time on earth ending as well. When Donovan raised his arm to the level, Jack felt his eye twitch. His arms hung limp at his side but his whole body was on alert, ready to explode into action.

Donovan opened his mouth for one last insult. "Don't worry. You won't be alone for too long. Eddie is going to send your girl to join you as soon as he has his money," he said. "Seems only fitting."

Jack ignored him, no more words would be spoken between them. His mental focus was entirely on the hammer of Donovan's gun. Once it clicked back, he would go. He figured Donovan would fire when he did, as a reflex, and the first bullet would miss, giving him at least a couple steps head start.

As Jack kept watch, a shot fired.

Jack flinched hard as a natural reaction to the sound, suspecting he had missed the signal and surely had been hit by a bullet. He looked down at his chest and waited for the blood to reveal where the bullet hit him, all the while his mind replaying the image of Donovan's gun. There had been no smoke, no recoil. It didn't add up. That couldn't have been Donovan's gun, he thought.

Jack turned his head back up towards Donovan. He was standing exactly as he had before, with exception to the ghastly look that had come over his face. His head and arm began to drop in unity. He was now the one looking down at his chest. He reached up with his other hand and found a hole right between his ribs. It was a perfect shot.

Donovan touched at the wound in his chest and then looked at the blood on his fingers, perplexed at what was happening. He looked up at Jack. A stream of blood came oozing out of his mouth. He looked like he wanted to say something, but instead he collapsed straight backwards, like a mighty tree felled to the ground. And into Jack's view as he went down was the glorious sight of Agent Travis, lined up directly behind him at nearly thirty yards away, firearm in hand.

"Nice shot, Agent Travis!" Jack yelled uncontrollably, feeling like he wanted to laugh and cry all at once.

Agent Travis didn't respond. He cautiously walked toward Donovan who was laying on his back, blinking up into the sun. When he reached Donovan, he put his foot down on Donovan's gun which had fallen not far from his hand. Agent Travis kept both hands firmly on his weapon as he inspected the situation. Jack hurried over to get his gun before joining him at Donovan's other side.

"What took you so long?" Jack said with a hint of sarcasm, his good fortune bringing with it a renewed sense of hope.

"Good to see you too, Jack," Agent Travis replied, his voice wavering from the excitement.

"How long have you been hiding in those trees?" Jack asked.

"All night," Agent Travis said, eyes still fixed on Donovan as he coughed out blood and struggled for breath.

"So it was you that followed Kate up here," Jack said.

"I'm in the FBI, Jack. It's called surveillance. It's what we do," Agent Travis replied with a hint of sarcasm of his own.

"Well, you're plenty good at it," Jack said, somewhat astonished at Agent Travis' skill given his own exhaustive search to find him the night before.

Donovan continued to spit up blood. He was conscious and had been listening to their conversation. Jack focused in on his eyes. Donovan had the look that he was up to something no good and Jack didn't look away.

Sure enough, in one final attempt, Donovan lurched towards his gun. He got a hold of the handle and pulled it out from under Travis's foot, causing him to fall off balance, his eyes growing wide with fear as he stumbled backwards.

But Jack was right on top of it, his gun springing out of the holster and firing once, hitting Donovan squarely. Donovan's arm hadn't come up far enough to fire a shot and it now dropped to the ground for the last time.

Agent Travis stood with his mouth wide open and a stunned look on his face. The action was so fast he hadn't had time to react. Once again, the perils of field work were staring him right between the eyes.

Jack holstered his gun and said, "Let's go," without hesitation or remorse, as he started to jog towards the trail Kate had lead Eddie and his remaining gang members along.

Knowing there was no time to waste, Agent Travis regrouped and followed after him, "Go where?" he asked.

"To Spring Hollow mine," Jack said, as he hurried ahead, anxious to make up lost ground on the gang.

Agent Travis worked to keep up, understanding the urgency of the situation. "I know Kate's in danger, but you and I are going to have to get on the same page if this is going to work," Travis said while they ran, their boots leaving a trail of dust as they proceeded towards the trees.

Jack thought about it. Agent Travis did have a point. He hadn't been entirely forthcoming with him a day earlier. Jack jumped over a rock in his path as he turned his head back towards Agent Travis and asked, "What do you need to know?"

Agent Travis didn't say anything at first. Jack kept up the swift pace. Travis was following closely behind with his gun still out and head turning in each direction. Both men began to labor with their breathing.

In a frustrated voice, Travis finally responded by calling out, "You didn't tell me you had the money."

"Would you have let me walk away if I had?" Jack called back. There was no time to mince words.

Agent Travis worked out his reply between breaths. "Regardless, you lied to me, Jack. If you want my help, you're going to have to do a lot better than that."

The two men kept running, their pace beginning to slow with fatigue.

"Did Kate know you were following her?" Jack finally said.

"No, I just told you it was surveillance."

"Deceit is another form of lying, Agent Travis" Jack said. "I'm gonna have to expect you do a lot better than that."

Agent Travis reached out and grabbed Jack's arm, stopping their progress. "Jack, we are heading into a hornet's nest here. I need to know I can trust you. Our lives are going to be in each other's hands."

Jack looked from Travis's hand and followed it up to find a sincere look on his face. Jack knew it was time to make peace, but it was also hard for him to put his trust in someone other than Kate. When he had tried that before, it usually ended badly. But given what he knew to this point about

Agent Travis, he concluded that he was a principled man. If he was ever going to trust anyone, now would be the time.

"You can," he said firmly, making sure that Agent Travis picked up the sincerity in his voice.

He leaned towards the trail to go before he stopped. While facing away from Travis, he said, "Agent Travis, I want to thank you for shooting Donovan."

He peeked back out of the corner of his eye to see Agent Travis's reaction. Travis had a sly smile on his face. "You know, I was just about to tell you the same thing."

Jack nodded and they were off again.

"How long until we reach the mine?" Travis asked.

Jack calculated before answering, "At this pace, we should be there in about five minutes."

"What are we going to do then?"

Jack answered as if he knew exactly what needed to happen. He said, "I'm going to get Kate, you're going to get the money, and Eddie is going to get what's coming to him."

25

As they raced towards the mine, Jack kept the rest of the conversation to a minimum. He could tell Agent Travis had more questions so Jack intentionally kept the pace brisk, forcing the men to breathe in lieu of talking. The terrain became easier as they went and they were making good time. It would only be another minute or two until they were within ear shot of the mine entrance. Jack put up his hand and slowed them down, preferring silence over speed as they approached.

"Are your concealment skills as good in the day as they are at night?" Jack asked in a hushed voice.

"They're fair. Although, I wish I had something other than this suit," said Travis.

Jack looked Agent Travis over, his expression acknowledging it wasn't the best way to remain camouflaged.

"Do you have a family?" Jack asked.

Agent Travis made a surprised look and whispered back, "Yeah, I do. A wife and a baby on the way."

Jack kept his eyes forward as they progressed slowly now, careful with each step not to make a noise. "What's your wife's name?" he said.

"Sarah," said Travis.

Jack stopped like he was contemplating the name before saying, "You should stay back a ways then. I'm sure Sarah wants you to come home tonight."

Agent Travis looked over at Jack with a surprised look that turned to gratitude. It made Jack uncomfortable so he turned the other direction and said, pointing, "Just around the corner will be the entrance to the mine. The trail goes hard to the left and then you are right on it. There will be tree cover the entire way but once you can see the mine entrance, anybody looking out of it will be able to see you."

He stopped speaking briefly, forming the plan as he spoke. "The way I figure it Eddie will have left Jimmy or Will or both behind to watch the entrance. There are other ways out of the mine but he doesn't know that so he must be planning to come out the way he went in. If that is the case, what I need to do is get close enough that I get the drop on them and not the other way around."

"How can I help, Jack? You don't have to do this alone," Travis said.

Jack didn't want to get Agent Travis killed but he knew he was right so Jack agreed to some help in a limited fashion.

"Ok, you hug the mountain side here on the left. Make your way as quietly as you can, always staying behind the rocks. I will head straight from here and once you see me turn sharp towards the mountain, that will be my signal so you'll know where the entrance to the mine is. At that point, try to bring it into view and then find a high spot where you can get off a few shots if needed. There are plenty of boulders along that side that should give you cover to make a safe position."

He watched as Agent Travis nodded nervously. Jack was nervous too but that didn't matter now. Kate was inside with Eddie and there was no time to spare.

Jack pulled out his gun and said, "Ready?"

"Wait. What about light? Do you have a flashlight once you get inside the mine?" Travis asked.

"There should be a few stashed inside the cave. Don't worry, I could walk it blindfolded if needed," before he asked again. "Are you ready?"

Agent Travis nodded again and Jack was off.

Jack worked his way through the brush, trying to stay concealed for as long as possible, he looked back to see Travis making his way to the rocks. As Jack gradually approached the mine entrance, he heard the sound of talking. Unless someone was talking to themselves, this wasn't welcome news. It meant he would likely have to face down Jimmy and

Will at the same time. Any advantage Jack had with his knowledge of the terrain was countered by the fact that these men were hardened criminals with a shoot first mentality.

Jack stayed hidden behind two rocks listening to the men so he could get a better handle on their locations. From what he could gather, one was behind the larger rocks on the left side of the entrance and the other was back in the entrance.

Jack looked around him, assessing his options for an approach. As he expected, it wasn't good. The path before him was a mix of larger pines and yellow rabbitbrush. The pines would shield him from incoming bullets but he might as well announce he's coming since they were deprived of any lower branches. The rabbitbrush, while a pretty part of Utah scenery with its small yellow flowers, was only tall enough to cover his boots and was therefore, useless. Jack was once again left contemplating a life or death run.

As he did, he watched Agent Travis work his way into position, rounding each rock carefully, looking to see if he was getting close. Jack had stopped moving south and made the left turn to signal the entrance of the mine but for some reason unbeknownst to Jack, Travis kept moving forward. He was now no more than 15 paces away from the entrance. Will and Jimmy were silent but near as Jack could tell that was a coincidence.

Jack tried to get his attention by signaling to him but Agent Travis had all of his energies focused on moving along the rocks without being seen or heard and didn't notice. He was now dangerously close to running face-to-face with the enemy.

Jack would have to find a better spot to signal to Travis. With a calculated guess that the men wouldn't yet be able to see him, he jumped out from behind the rocks and pressed his back to a tree. As he did, he caught a glimpse of Will out of the corner of his eye, leaning against the rock to the left of the entrance, which meant Jimmy was the one in the entrance. He slowly poked his head around the tree to make sure Will hadn't noticed him. As far as he could tell, he hadn't.

He turned back to Agent Travis who had seen him make his jump and was now looking directly at him. Jack gave him a frenzied look and nodded in the direction of the opening, trying to show him how close he was to it. Travis looked back and forth from Jack to the rocks in front of him, leaning out in an attempt to look around them. Eventually, he put up his hands to show Jack that he understood him, backing up in the process.

Unfortunately as he did, he kicked a rock about the size of a baseball that went rolling down the slope. It seemed to Jack to hit every other rock on its way down before landing in the brush. Agent Travis froze and looked to Jack, eyes wide.

Jack's heart stopped cold. He peeked again and sure enough, Will had heard it. He had drawn his gun and was looking in the direction of the exposed FBI Agent, only a large boulder between them.

Jack signaled for Agent Travis to try again to move back, adding his finger over his lips to call for silence. Travis started back again slowly, worry in every step, as Will began to advance cautiously, still unsure of who or what was behind the rock. Jack reached down to the handle of his revolver. Whatever was about to happen was likely to be quick.

Will breached the rock and stared into the place Agent Travis was standing just moments ago, gun forward and ready to shoot. It was empty. He looked around confused, knowing he had heard something.

"What is it?" Jimmy called out.

Will didn't answer. Instead, he went back to tracking forward around the next turn. Jack could see Agent Travis had taken up position behind that rock. He had nowhere left to go. If he tried to push back further to the next rock, he would be exposed to Will before he made it. If he stayed put, Will would find him. It was a no win situation.

Jack had to think fast. With Will abandoning his post, maybe he could cause a distraction at the mine entrance, he thought. He felt confident in his ability to take Jimmy on one-on-one, even in a shootout. This might be enough to get Will to reverse course and give Agent Travis a chance.

Jack peeked out again, looking at the mine entrance for Jimmy. He could see him now, sticking his head out into the sun tentatively, calling on occasion for Will who still wasn't answering. Jack glanced back to Will. He was moments away from coming face-to-face with Agent Travis. He had to act now.

Jack lifted his revolver and steadied his hands around it as he leaned around the side of the tree, bringing Jimmy into his sights. It was a difficult shot with a handgun and his target was fidgeting between the light of the sun and the blackness of the tunnel. His years of practice on shooting rabbits from less than ideal positions was about to be tested.

He took one more glance over to Will and Agent Travis before relocating his target and squeezing off a shot, breaking the silence in the process.

With a jerk of his neck and a splatter of blood, Jimmy dropped from Jack's view. His shot had found its mark.

Unfortunately, he was now exposed to Will who had wheeled around and began unloading his gun frantically in Jack's direction. Jack rolled to the other side of the tree to put it in between him and Will's bullets. He could feel them as they impacted the tree, bark flying off around him. He tried to look around to see what was going on but the shots kept Jack pinned down, that is, until he heard the click of an empty gun.

Jack leapt to the next tree, stealing a look in Will's direction. Will jumped behind the boulder where Travis had originally been. Jack didn't know how much time he would have before Will could reload. He rushed forward, gun out, arm extended, bouncing between the trees, trying to close as much distance as he could before Will started shooting again. As he did, Agent Travis emerged from behind his rock.

"Drop your weapon!" Travis exclaimed, pointing his gun at Will at close range.

This startled Jack. Not so much that Agent Travis had made a move, but that he was asking Will to give up. Maybe killing Donovan was all he could stand in a day's work. Maybe he wanted a suspect alive to take back downtown. Either way, Jack was unsettled by it. He didn't expect Will was going to comply.

Running full speed towards Travis, Jack kept his eyes up as the scene unfolded before him. He couldn't see Will as he was shielded by the rock, but he knew he was directly in front of Travis, no more than seven or eight feet away. He saw Agent Travis, with his arm mostly extended, reiterate the command. Then he watched as Travis pushed his gun towards Will and fired.

He heard multiple shots, too many to come from one gun. He watched as Agent Travis slumped over, reaching for a rock to stabilize himself. No more shots were fired. It was all over in a blink of an eye.

Jack got there just in time to catch Travis before he slid off the rock to the ground, leaving a trail of blood against the boulder. Jack could now see Will. It was clear he was dead. Jack tossed his gun to the ground and helped Agent Travis into a soft landing on the dirt. He looked him over.

Travis was favoring his right shoulder. Jack pressed his hand under his suit coat until he felt the warm flow of blood exiting his body.

"I'm alright," Agent Travis said with a pained look.

"You're hit, but the bullet went through," Jack said relieved. "We need to stop the bleeding but I think you will live."

Jack helped Agent Travis out of his suit coat and then ripped off a strip that he could use to hold against the wound. "Hold this tight," he said, as he pushed the rest of the jacket under his shoulder.

"So much for staying out of harm's way," Jack said, trying to keep the situation light and keep the Agent's spirits up.

It worked. Travis produced a faint smile. He was hurting, but he was breathing and blinking his eyes. Jack took this as a good sign.

"You need to go," Agent Travis said, blinking several times as a bead of sweat dropped into his eye. "You need to go save Kate."

Jack paused from treating Agent Travis's wound to look at him. He could tell the offer for Jack to leave was sincere.

"Help me up," Agent Travis said as he winced in pain as he grabbed Jack's shoulder with his one good arm. "If you can get me to a position just outside the entrance of the mine, I will make sure Eddie doesn't get past me if he tries to escape."

Jack was surprised but glad to hear it. Agent Travis was still in the fight. Jack could feel his optimism growing as a faint smile crossed his face.

"Stop smiling. It hurts my shoulder," Agent Travis said in a joking manner. "Just get me up."

Jack helped Travis up and moved him to a spot near where Will had been guarding the entrance, except Travis was right against the mountain, concealing himself from anyone who would be exiting the mine.

"Jack," Agent Travis said as Jack rearranged the makeshift bandage. "If you have to, give up the money. Drive him out to me. I will finish him."

"Agent Travis, that doesn't sound like the words of law enforcement," Jack said ironically.

"Well," Agent Travis responded, "sometimes things aren't always black and white, but they do still come down to right and wrong," quoting Jack from the day prior.

He gave Jack an encouraging look and said with a renewed determination, "Now go get your girl."

With Travis in position, Jack didn't hesitate. After dragging Jimmy out of the entrance to clear a path, he hurried back towards the Spring Hollow Mine entrance. He had made this walk many times before, but never with such purpose. He didn't know how, but he knew he had to be prepared to do whatever it took to bring Kate out alive. Without another word to Agent Travis, he disappeared into the pitch black.

26

Kate blinked repeatedly as she and Eddie entered into the mine, her eyes trying to adjust in the dark. The cold air, immediately present, gave her goosebumps. But that was still more welcome than Eddie's hand grasped tightly around her arm. The anxiety of being caught in the midst of her two worst nightmares was intensifying and the shock of hearing two gunshots had yet to fade. But if she was going to survive, she couldn't give in to her fears. She tried to refocus her mind.

"How are we going to see anything?" Eddie protested loudly as he squeezed harder on her arm. That brought Kate to attention.

"Over here," she said, moving further into the mine. "This is where we keep the lights." She fumbled along the wall until she felt the shelf-like opening that had been carved out at about shoulder height. She felt over the two old flashlights sitting on the dusty shelf until she found the lantern. It was the brightest option available and she preferred as much light as possible if she was to be alone with Eddie.

After stoking the lantern, she lit the match and placed it inside the globe, hoping it would light. A glow slowly began to brighten until it reached its full potential. She discarded the match and grabbed the lantern by the bail. The light bounced shadows off the walls, which made Eddie's face look even more terrifying than before. She stood silently, waiting for him to give his next order.

"Well, take me to it," he said with an impatient look. "I didn't come all this way for nothing."

His eyes were wild in his lust for money. At least, Kate hoped that was what he was lusting after. She couldn't help but to swallow loudly as she turned, struggling to keep her composure. She held up the lamp as she looked down the tunnel. A wave of memories flooded back from the many times she had been here before. It felt overwhelming. She still struggled to take that next step.

Stay calm, she told herself. That's what Jack would do. He would stay calm and come up with a plan. There has to be a way to get out of here alive. If Jack were here, he would find…

Her inner thoughts came to a halt with the sudden realization of what she had to do. Her mind quickly went to work formulating her plan. It wasn't foolproof, everything would have to go just right, but it might just work, she thought.

When she was ready, she looked back up at Eddie and said, "This way."

Kate felt Eddie let go of her arm and she walked forward a few paces while he stayed back. She didn't know what he was up to but she glanced back while making the first turn. She could see he was moving forward with her now, closing the distance. He had his shotgun held in front of him with both hands, the muzzle pointing right at her.

"Just so there's no funny business," he said with a sneer.

Kate walked on, slowly counting and thinking and whispering quietly as she went. It wasn't a ploy or a trick, she was doing her best to remember how far to each turn so she could end up in the right place. The mine had several miles worth of runs, all connecting at different intersections. Those runs came across openings and rooms, some with makeshift tables and useless gear long since abandoned.

The tunnels themselves were braced with railroad ties every dozen feet. The wall had a metal pipe secured near the ceiling that went along the main run to send electricity to the deep recesses of the mine, but the power had long since been shut off and now it served only as a marker to let her know when she was on the main path.

Kate and Eddie walked in silence, which was just fine with her. She could hear his slow wheezing behind her. It told her when he was close. She tried to keep some distance between them, but at times she had to stop to get her bearings. When she did she could feel his breath as it intermixed with her hair. It gave her the creeps so she quickly pressed on, her knees trembling and threatening to give way.

After several minutes of walking, Eddie grew impatient. Kate had to stop to consider a turn when she felt the hard steel of his gun press into her lower back.

"You sure you know where you're going? `Cause you don't look like you know where you're going," Eddie said, his voice shifting to a low growl.

"Yes, I think so," Kate responded, stepping forward slowly to remove herself from contact with the shotgun as she turned to face him.

"You think so!" Eddie blurted back at her with a derisive laugh. "Doll, you're gonna have to do a heck of a lot better than I think so," he said as he moved closer to her, backing her into the wall.

"I know where it is," she promised nervously, as she put up her hand as if that would stop him.

He continued forward until her hand made contact with his stomach. The feeling was more unpleasant then she might have imagined. She closed her eyes and turned away as she did, the lantern hanging low in her other hand, its light being cutoff as he advanced. She could feel him leaning into her. She could smell his stench. Eddie stood silent for several seconds, seeming to enjoy her hand being forced to touch him.

To Kate, time seemed multiplied and she wondered when he would let her go. Not just from being pressed between him and the dirty mine shaft wall, but from the torment of his company. His wretched, deplorable presence in her life stood in stark contrast of her goodness. It was as if light was competing against dark, and the darkness was winning. She knew if she was to make it out alive that she would soon have to fight back, using the cold darkness to her advantage.

"Let's go then," Eddie finally said while he kept himself pressed against her. "But it better be close by, for your sake."

Kate didn't look up as she slid past him, preferring to scrape her back against the wall versus making any further contact with Eddie. As she did, she started to feel lightheaded. The shadows dancing on the walls only added to her dizziness. She brought her hand up to her temples.

She felt like she might collapse but she fought the urge, knowing that could prove even more costly. Who knows what Eddie would do to me, she thought. She tried to regain her bearings and continue with her plan when she felt a tap from Eddie's shotgun against her arm, a not-so-friendly reminder to keep moving.

She held the light up as she looked down the run to her left. She peered extra hard while confirming the path. It looked familiar. Without saying a word, she walked forward. Her boots slapped the ground with each step as she headed down an inclined run that led to an opening at the bottom. She could hear the faint sound of water leaking through the rock. As they entered into the opening, she held the lantern higher and looked around. She had found the spot she was looking for.

The room was large at about 30 feet per side. The ceiling got higher as she walked towards the center. It was easily ten feet tall. There was a slow but steady drip of water that came from the back of the room, breaking the silence with its methodical sound. There was no way in or out, other than the way they had come.

One thing Eddie was sure to notice was the room was devoid of any other worldly objects, including bags of money. She watched him as he looked around, wondering what the catch was. He held his shotgun on Kate and made sure she stayed out in front of him. She could tell by the grimace on his face that he wasn't happy.

"I ain't seeing what I ought to be seeing," Eddie muttered as he continued to look around intently.

Kate stood in the middle of the room, holding the lantern up. Eddie walked slowly towards her. She held her ground. Just as he started to protest again, they heard a shot fired in the distance.

This brought Eddie to a halt. Kate was startled too. Eddie turned with a quizzical look, trying to decipher what was happening up above. They waited in silence. More shots were heard, off and on. Then the silence returned for good. Neither one of them knew quite what to make of it.

"Don't you pay no mind to that," Eddie said staunchly. "Them boys get trigger happy sometimes. It's all for the fun of it."

Kate didn't know what to think but she grasped on to the thin possibility that Jack was still alive, that he was coming for her. It may have been wishful thinking, but it was just the motivation she needed for what she was about to do.

"What exactly is this place?" Eddie said directly, as he waved his shotgun around like a wand.

Kate looked around again. She honestly had no idea what the room was originally used for. But she remembered it well. The last time she saw this room, in the light, was in the moments leading up to when she had dropped and broken her flashlight as a young girl. She could still remember struggling on hands and knees to make her way up the run, trying to find her way out, being lost until she was found by Jack. The memory of this room had haunted her plenty over the years. On that day, it was the moment of her greatest personal agony.

But today, she felt different than she did back then. Today, she would get revenge on both of her nightmares. Agony was about to turn into redemption. Today, Eddie would be the one left in the dark.

27

Eddie turned around, looking more angry than scared by her unwillingness to answer him. He was only a few steps away from her in the middle of the room, his eyes large with rage.

"Give me my money!" he yelled with all his might as he leaned in towards her. She closed her eyes as his thundering words rolled over her.

She opened her eyes. Her chest was heaving and her lips trembling as she answered him, "That's all you care about, isn't it? It doesn't matter to you how many lives you ruin. How many people you kill? You only care about yourself. Well, I have news for you, it's not your money, and I wouldn't give it to you even if I did know where it was!"

With that, Kate slammed the lantern down hard into the ground, breaking the glass to pieces. The mantle quickly went out, the cold dark taking back the mine.

She heard Eddie roar as he lunged forward at her. She had quietly taken two steps back and several steps to the side careful not to lose her bearings towards the exit. Silence and precision would be the key to her escape. She quietly made her way to the entrance of the room, arms outstretched in front of her, as Eddie tore through a string of expletives that echoed off of every wall.

The sound was deafening to her ears, but provided excellent cover for her feet. Her mind raced as she hoped she could remember all the turns and distances she had memorized along the way.

She found the wall and kept her hand lightly on it as she felt her feet start up the ascent of the run, counting steps in her head. She could hear

Eddie struggling and yelling back in the room. She knew how quickly he would become disoriented in the dark. Her heart was swelling with a terrible combination of hope and fear. She wanted to yell for Jack but she had no way of knowing if he was coming. And if she did, she would give away her position to Eddie so she kept quiet, holding her other hand over her heart in an attempt to keep it in her chest.

As the wall began to widen to her left, she felt her feet hit level ground. She had made it up the run and was about to turn when a faint light came from behind her. She turned to look. It was Eddie holding up a cigarette lighter, down at the bottom of the tunnel.

"I ain't through with you yet," he said with a snarl as he held the light up to his face for her to see.

Kate's hand dropped from her chest. Her heart skipped a beat.

She had no choice but to keep going forward as fast as she could into the darkness of the tunnel, heading back towards the entrance. She could hear Eddie laugh as she went. She had almost no light except for the tiny amount from Eddie's lighter. Even then, when there was extra light to help her see it only meant he was getting closer. Fortunately, the incline proved to be a challenge for him. His wheezing grew louder as he struggled up that stretch of the tunnel.

Kate's mind was in a panic. She was doing her best to remember the sequence of turns and the number of railroad ties to pass before her next turn. Her thoughts betrayed her as they kept backsliding to the idea that she wouldn't make it far before Eddie would catch her. She knew she would soon have to find a place to hide.

She felt her hand glide over the third railroad tie, which meant it was time for a right turn. She glanced back and could hear Eddie as he was about to round the corner to her corridor. She made a gut decision and went left instead, vaguely remembering a thin closet-like space carved out for tools not far away.

She made her way to the space by feeling along the wall as quiet as she could and slid into it. It was barely wide enough for her to fit. If Eddie went that way, she would surely be trapped.

She stayed perfectly still and listened. Eddie wheezed his way into the intersection and stopped, confronted with a choice. He could keep going straight, turn to the right (which would lead back towards the entrance), or to the left where Kate was hiding about twenty feet away. Kate breathed softly with her hands near her face and waited.

"I'll go easy on you if you come out now," Eddie said with his villainous voice. "Otherwise, there will be a debt to pay…and I will collect."

The light from the hallway was fluctuating as Eddie had to relight his lighter several times. It was having trouble staying lit. Kate was glad for it, as it evened the playing field, but she didn't have time to relish in it as she had a developing problem of her own. She felt a sneeze coming on.

Likely due to the dust she stirred up while sliding into her hiding spot, something was there, tickling at the inside of her nose. She did her best to fight it, ironically attempting to calm the God-given reflex meant to protect her body. Silently, she put one hand tightly over her mouth and with the other she pinched her nose.

The sneeze hung in the balance for several seconds, trying to decide whether or not to make an appearance. Slowly, the scale began to tip – she was losing it. Once the line had been crossed, there was no stopping it. She braced her back against the wall, pushed her feet out against the other and held on with all her might.

When it came Kate felt her eyes expand and her ears pop. She heard a slight gust of air exit through her fingers. It was noticeable to her, but was it noticeable to Eddie? If he had heard it, he hadn't yet taken a step. She waited to see if there would be an encore but thankfully, none came.

Eddie continued to fumble with his lighter and then walked off in a different direction. Kate leaned out to see the light coming from the middle path. Eddie had chosen to go straight forward. Kate waited until his steps were distant before making her way back to the intersecting tunnels. She tip-toed through it and returned to her course, relieved to be heading closer to the entrance.

Kate continued her routine of gliding her hands along the wall, counting railroad ties as they passed. She had memorized them as 4-L, 2-R, 6-L, which stood for the number of railroad ties and the direction to turn. It was painstaking progress as she had to make sure to be perfectly silent, not lose track of her count, and to decipher her clues in reverse. One wrong turn meant she was lost, with no way to get back on track. All the while she continued to fight the urge to yell for Jack.

On occasion, she would hear Eddie walking and cursing, a stark reminder she wasn't out of the woods yet. She was careful to stop and look around often to make sure she didn't see a light. The tunnels were interconnected so it was not safe to assume that he would only show up from behind. She had to guard against every direction.

She was down to only three sequences of numbers left when she paused. Three more turns until she would see the entrance. She knew that she likely couldn't go out that way if Eddie's men were still standing guard, but it would provide her context to where she was in the mine. If she could get back to that point, she knew a safe exit not far away through an inclined ventilation shaft. It would be a tight squeeze but one she expected to fit through. Even better was the fact that she would come out on the right side of the mountain so that she wouldn't have to pass back across the entrance once out.

But as Kate came up to the next intersection, she heard it. It was Eddie's footsteps and he was close. She froze, not knowing what to do. Should she run? She wondered if she could make it, and if doing so would reveal her to the other gang members. The sound was getting closer. She could hear the lighter striking over and over again but she could see no light. The time for a decision was up. She would have to go back.

Kate fumbled along the walls in retreat as best as she could, but it wasn't good enough. In her haste she was no longer silent. As she came around the corner of the intersection, she ran right smack into Eddie. Kate let out a cry.

"Where do you think you're going?" Eddie scoffed, as he grabbed her by the shoulders and held her roughly.

She struggled as he pushed her into an adjacent room off the corner of the intersection. Her momentum carried her forward into the wall. Eddie stood at the entrance, breathing heavily and leaving no room for escape. Kate was trapped.

It took Eddie several seconds to catch his breath before he could speak, each gasp sounding an alarm to Kate.

"Not smart girlie. I gave you a chance, a chance to be fair to me, and again you tried to leave me for dead. Tried to best old Eddie." He paused to wheeze in some more air. "Well you're out of chances now. If you don't have my money, I guess I'll have to take something else," Eddie said with a fiendish grin.

Kate leaned back against the wall. Her hands were down by her waist, pressed hard against the rock, as she muttered, "Oh God," subconsciously under her breath.

"Sure, you can call me that," Eddie snapped back. "In fact, why don't you scream that for me while I break into you," he said as he slowly advanced towards her methodically to maximize her fear.

Kate prepared for the worst, her hopes of escape were cut down just short. Her eyes darted around the room but it was too small. She had no way to get around him. Eddie smiled a disgusting smile as he came closer. Once in reach, he lunged at her, pinning her against the wall. She gave off a horrified scream as his lighter dropped to the ground and bounced away, the light going out in the process.

She was alone in the dark, fighting against the devil himself.

28

Jack walked through the dark, his hands feeling along the rock, looking for the hole in the wall that held the flashlights. When he came to it, he felt around on the ledge until he found them. The lantern was missing and Kate was sure to have taken it. He tried the first flashlight. Dead. "Shoot," he said angrily as he tossed it back on shelf. He grabbed at the second, his last hope for light while he searched the mine.

"I'll do this without you if I have to," he said stubbornly to the dinged up metal flashlight in his hand as he clicked the switch. Fortunately, light came streaming out enthusiastically, as if its sole purpose was to lead the way to Kate. "Thank heavens," Jack said relieved as he pointed it down the tunnel, the dust reflecting in the light as it danced around in the air.

The site of the tunnel brought Jack a strange sense of relief. He loved this mine. He knew it inside and out. He felt a surge of energy as he started forward.

He jogged down the tunnel, doing his best to listen while he went. Soon enough, he was at the first intersection and had a decision to make. He knew the money was hidden down the tunnel to the right, but that didn't necessarily mean that was where he would find Kate. Quite frankly, Eddie could have taken her anywhere in the mine.

As he stood calculating a decision on the path to take, he heard Kate scream. Her scream was filled with such horror that Jack literally recoiled from the sound of it, feeling its full effect as it tore into him. The only good it held was to tell him which direction to go, and that she wasn't far away.

Jack gathered himself and ran in a full sprint in the direction of the sound. He could hear a commotion but couldn't tell yet exactly where it was coming from. He ran up and down each tunnel, stopping to check any openings along the way. He knew he was close but he couldn't find her. The sounds of screams and commotion had stopped, leaving him no other way of knowing where she was.

He stopped at the next intersection and turned off the light, listening. Still nothing. After a few seconds, he yelled, "Kate!"

The sound of his voice echoed throughout the mine, slowly fading after several repetitions, but there was no response. He listened some more, the sound of his own breathing the only sound available. He yelled for her again. This time he heard movement coming directly behind him.

He wheeled around, pulled his gun and turned on the light. There in the hallway, directly in front of him, stood Fast Eddie, holding Kate in front of him with one hand over her mouth and the other holding his shotgun out from under her arm, pointing it up to the side of her head. Kate's hands were grasping at the one Eddie used to cover her mouth, but she couldn't get him to let go. The stillness of the Spring Hollow mine was broken as Eddie maneuvered them forward towards Jack.

"I must say I am surprised to see you, Boy," Eddie said. "You must have some kind of story to tell if you escaped from Donovan."

"Not really," Jack replied, not willing to let Eddie control the situation. "It was easy once he was dead."

Eddie furrowed his brow in ire, his temperament quickly reverting to his depraved nature. "Boy, I ought to let you have it right now," he said as he turned his shotgun towards Jack, both men now pointing their weapons at each other.

"But then how would you find your money?" Jack said, knowing he had to think fast. It would be too easy for Eddie to pull the trigger while Jack had no shot in return with Eddie using Kate as a human shield.

"If I had a dollar for every time you two told me that, I would already be a rich man," Eddie replied. "That's not going to work with me anymore. Someone's going to pay up right now or she gets it," he said as he turned the gun back on Kate.

Kate let out a muffled scream, breathing frantically through her nose as Eddie pushed the gun up under her jaw. She tried to reach for the shotgun but Eddie pinned her arms back with his elbows. She was defenseless. Jack watched as Kate's eyes grew wide before she shut them tight and braced for the impact.

Immediately, Jack threw his gun on the ground to intervene. "There, you can have it." He watched as Eddie glanced down to the gun sliding up to his feet. "I will trade you the money for the girl right now."

Eddie's face was stuck in an angry sneer. He hardened his eyes into a squint as he pressed the gun up harder into Kate, forcing her head back.

"And I can have the money here in five minutes," Jack said in an attempt to sweeten the offer.

Jack could see Eddie contemplating the situation. As much as he likely wanted to finish both of them on the spot, his first love was still the money. In the end, Jack's proposition had worked. The shotgun was lowered and was pointed back to Jack.

"Five minutes, and not a second more," Eddie said, his face now changing to one of distress more than anger. Jack could see even the mighty Eddie was wearing down.

"But she is not to be touched," Jack said pointing at Kate. "If I come back and she was harmed in anyway while I am gone, the deal's off. I just keep moving and you never see this money again."

Eddie stood there, mulling over the deal again. Jack could see Eddie didn't like being told what he would or wouldn't do. Still the answer came as expected.

"Go get my money," Eddie said in a calm-like manner, as he removed his hand from Kate's mouth and slid it down her torso to her arm, making sure not to let his collateral get far away.

Kate's face was filled with anguish. Jack gave her a reassuring look and then headed swiftly down the tunnel. "Five minutes," he heard Eddie yell after him.

Jack went with a purpose, knowing exactly where the money was. He could get to it and be back in five minutes, no problem. The challenge was what to do when he got back. His thoughts mobilized around this dilemma. He had to come up with some sort of counterattack. He had no gun, and no way to protect Kate. Whatever he would come up with, it had to be good. There would be no margin for error.

Jack went along a curved path in the mountain until he saw what he was looking for, light from the outside, shining down through a ventilation shaft. There, not five yards past it, was a pile of discarded rocks against a wall where the path widened out.

Jack walked straight to it, placing the flashlight on the ground to provide light in the right direction, and began taking rocks off the pile, carelessly throwing them aside. He worked feverishly, throwing rocks at a rapid pace. As the pile grew smaller he dropped to his knees, using both hands to push rocks off until he felt the textured canvass material on his fingertips. There they were. Two bags filled with money that hadn't seen the light of day in nearly two years.

Jack worked them free and dropped them in the middle of the tunnel. He stood over them, catching his breath, the light from the flashlight casting his shadow on the wall. His time would be more than half up by now. He had to get moving.

He picked up both bags with one arm and heaved them up to his shoulder, which caused him to pitch forward from their considerable weight. He reached down to pick up his flashlight when he saw something out of the corner of his eye, lying against the wall, partially hidden by loose rocks.

He walked over and picked up the object, inspecting it closely. After a lengthy pause to consider the plan forming in his mind, he shoved the item under his other arm and headed off, back to face his adversary.

The journey back checked Jack in the gut. He knew that in a matter of seconds, someone was going to die. There were no two ways about it. Either he would kill Eddie or Eddie would kill him, and probably Kate too. There was no common ground to be found, only confrontation. He made sure this point was clear in his mind. Any hesitation, any reluctance, would only serve to lessen his chances. As he walked back to face Fast Eddie—the brute that poured ruin over his past, present and future—he loaded all the pain and anguish Eddie had caused like ammunition into a gun, and held it by a hairpin trigger just under the surface.

He shifted the bags, the flashlight, and the item to more advantageous positions as he approached the intersection where he left Kate and Eddie. He could see the faint light of Eddie's lighter as he approached. Kate stood next to him, but at arm's length, Eddie still holding her by the upper arm.

Eddie watched intently as Jack approached and dropped the bags of money to the ground, one after another, making a loud thud in the process. A smile came over Eddie's face as if he had found a lost loved one. He pointed his shotgun up at Jack, and said, "Throw me that flashlight." Jack tossed it to him. Eddie let go of Kate's arm as he caught it and moved towards the bags.

"Step back and put your hands up high where I can see them," Eddie told Jack.

Jack complied by taking the smallest two steps back he could and putting his hands up, resting them lightly on the top of his head. Kate had moved to the wall and began slowly sliding towards Jack.

Eddie was already kneeling next to the money bags when he pointed a finger from his meaty hand in her direction, and said, "Stay right there, Doll," never once looking up while he grabbed at the zipper on the bag. He paused like he was worshipping in front of a sacred altar, taking in the sanctity of the situation.

He grabbed the zipper and pulled. It made a loud whoosh as he whisked it from one end of the bag to the other, the cash pushing its way up to crest over the edge in the process. Eddie flashed a perverted smile as he reached down to grab a stack of hundreds. He smacked it against his inner thigh to knock off the dust and held it up into the light. He looked at the money like his exaltation had been achieved.

Jack looked over to Kate. She was holding onto the wall looking back at him. She was no more than five steps away on his right. Jack's lips were closed but he sent her a trusting look while he nodded his head slightly, shifting his eyes to Eddie and then back to her. Kate glanced down to Eddie and back to Jack. She looked afraid but Jack could see she understood.

Eddie was busy opening the second bag to check its contents, his other hand holding the shotgun on Jack, who was standing directly in front of him at a distance of six feet. Jack watched, surprised that he wasn't given more attention considering he had already bested Donovan.

But Eddie was engrossed by the money, feeling deeper into the bag. This caused him to miss the fact that Jack was quietly sliding his right hand behind his back, reaching for the lead pipe that was running up the length of his spine, suspended in his belt behind him.

29

One of Jack's favorite past times growing up was to watch the Spring storms roll in over the Wellsville mountains to the west of Logan. He would sit by his window at night and watch them come, bringing fierce winds and rains. He wasn't so much interested in the rain or wind as he was the lightning. He would watch intently in an effort to see where the lightning started and how it moved as it raced to the ground. He wanted to see it shift and bend as it created its random path to earth.

The problem is, he could never see the process in action. By the time he saw the lightning begin, it had already reached the ground, and had made several changes in direction along the way to create its crooked line. No matter how closely he watched, and how many thousands of times he had seen it, he never once deciphered its moves. It was simply too fast. As Jack wrapped his fingers around the rusty, one-inch diameter pipe behind him, all of his thoughts were focused on how to move like lightning. How to shift and bend and crash, all in an instant.

Jack drew in his final breath, preparing to go on the exhale. As his lungs reached their pinnacle, Jack exploded forward, unlocking all of his rage in one fluid motion, stepping right and then crashing the metal rod down into Eddie's head with all his might.

Eddie fired immediately, his gun blasting away at the silence, but hitting nothing else. The shotgun dropped from his hands. Jack continued with blow after blow as Eddie rolled onto his back in a defensive position.

Jack continued to make contact but Eddie was deflecting many of Jack's strikes away from serious injury with his arms. The flashlight rolled off the money bag as Jack worked the lead pipe around Eddie's body. He connected several more times, but the first strike to Eddie's head was the only clean hit. He knew he would have to inflict more damage before Eddie would be stopped.

Jack glanced down and saw his gun sticking out of Eddie's belt. He wondered if he should drop the pipe and reach for it, knowing a few well-placed shots would end the conflict. As he swung down again, Eddie was able to grab a hold of the other end of the pipe. It turned into a tug-o-war. Jack abandoned hope of getting his gun as they jerked the pipe back-and-forth violently between them.

By Eddie's second pull Jack could feel his arms being stretched from his shoulders. He was no match in strength for this kind of contest with Eddie, even after the blow to his head. By Eddie's third pull, Jack let go to avoid being pulled to the ground.

Jack watched as the pipe bounced into the corner, slipping from Eddie's hand when Jack no longer resisted. With his hands free, Eddie moved for the pistol in his waistband. Thinking quick, Jack kicked at his pistol as Eddie pulled it from his trousers. It went flying end-over-end behind them into the dark.

Both men stole a glance over to the shotgun. It lay on the other side of the bags, the break action open with no sign of the second shell. It must have bounced free when the gun hit the ground, Jack thought. Eddie saw it too and made no move for it.

Jack stood ready but was unsure how to attack. He remembered why they called him Fast Eddie. If Jack made a move to the pistol or the pipe, it would likely end with Eddie crashing down on him from behind. When nothing came to mind, he relinquished the next move to Eddie.

Eddie rolled over and slowly climbed his way to his feet, keeping an eye on Jack the entire way up. His balance had clearly been affected as he wobbled momentarily and struggled to stay upright. His wheezing had grown worse. He sounded more like a snake hissing than a man breathing.

Jack glanced back at Kate. It appeared she hadn't moved from her original spot but somehow she had the flashlight. It must have been kicked towards her. She was holding the light on Eddie, and Jack shifted over to stand guard in front of her while he waited for the fight to resume.

Eddie reached up to feel the gash on his head. Jack could see a fluid working its way down through Eddie's hair towards his forehead. As he pulled his fingers down, they were red with blood. Eddie showed it to Jack and said, “Take a good look. That’s all you get. The rest is coming from you.”

Jack held his ground, fists up, unflinching from Eddie’s threats.

“Huh,” Eddie laughed as he looked over his opponent. “You ain’t man enough, Boy. Haven’t you learned that by now?”

Jack stayed ready.

He watched as Eddie said, “Guess not,” as he wiped the blood on his shirt.

“You must be one of those slow learners. I’ll help you learn it good.” Eddie said as he swiped at Jack from the side like a cat, with his palm open, trying to grab him. Jack skirted it. Eddie paused and swiped again. Jack again moved back but he was quickly running out of room to maneuver if he was to protect Kate.

Eddie smiled, realizing Jack’s predicament. He started forward again when everything suddenly went black. Kate had turned off the light. Jack took advantage and switched his position in the dark as Eddie cursed. A second later the light came back on and Jack gashed Eddie with an uppercut to the chin from his stance at Eddie’s side. Eddie swung back but the light went out again before he could hit his target.

Jack repositioned himself again, this time behind Eddie. The light came back on and Jack gave him a flurry of kidney shots before the light went off. This time Jack didn’t know where Eddie was so he laid back, waiting for the light.

As the light came on again, Eddie had moved to Kate’s position. He lunged at her and caught just enough of her sleeve to keep her close. She struggled to free herself as she tried to move away. Jack saw Eddie reaching with his other hand to secure her.

With no time to think, Jack rushed at them, brushing by Kate as he tackled Eddie head on. Jack drove forward, his head buried in Eddie’s chest as he wrapped him up and pushed him back. Kate had managed to break free but Jack was in an unwelcome position, wrestling Eddie with everything he had.

It didn’t take long for Eddie to turn the tide and begin to push him back. Jack dug in his heels but despite leveraging up every muscle he had, Eddie was just too strong. He gradually pushed Jack backwards until he was up against the wall, pounding him hard against the rocks in the process.

Jack grimaced. He held Eddie by the shoulders and tried to push off the rocks but it was in vain. Eddie pushed him back again, punishing him with the rock wall. Jack tried to squirm off to the right, and then the left, but Eddie had his hands on each shoulder and pinned him back with each attempt. He had no way out.

Eddie continued bouncing Jack off the wall, his head and neck taking the toll. With every violent shake, Jack's hopes for a happy ending grew dimmer. But despite the drubbing he was taking, Jack never said a word. No plea for mercy, no begging. Instead he struggled on, committed to fighting to his last breath.

Jack wondered how long he could keep this up, until his will would break. He looked over Eddie's shoulder to get one last look at Kate before he left this world for the next and to his surprise, the girl who had snuck up on him the day they met, was up to it again. She was about to offer him one last chance for survival.

With a flashlight in one hand and Jack's pistol in the other, she stepped into position behind them, angled slightly off to one side. And she was surprisingly close too, at no more than ten feet from them.

Eddie noticed Jack had shifted his attention and spun around, remembering now that there was someone else in the room.

"That's enough," Kate said, her voice trembling but her hand steady.

Jack slumped against the wall but kept his eyes fixed on Kate. Eddie had yet to move, careful not to provoke her. His hands hung at his sides as he contemplated his next move. The mine went silent again.

As Jack watched Kate holding the gun, he could see she was nervous. Eddie was sure to see it too. He was likely betting against her being able to finish it. But not Jack. There was no question in his mind she would pull that trigger.

And as soon as Eddie moved to square up to Kate, she fired, without hesitation, blowing a hole right through the middle of his chest. Eddie staggered back, clutching at his chest. Kate held the gun on him, prepared to fire again, as he fell backwards to the ground. Eddie landed hard on his back, with arms and legs extended.

Jack got up and stumbled over to Kate, taking the gun from her now trembling hand. Jack lowered her arm softly. She looked up to him with glossy eyes. He held her stare, wanting to comfort her, but he had one more thing to do before it could be finished.

He walked slowly over to Eddie, his head throbbing with each step. Eddie lay on the ground where he fell, looking up at the ceiling, wheezing his final breaths. To Jack he looked no less menacing even while he lay there dying. He wondered if Kate's shot had ended him or if he would have to fire again.

Jack raised the gun from his side and cocked the trigger while aiming it at Eddie as a precaution.

Then Eddie did what he has always done best, he talked. Looking at Jack defiantly while blood was seeping through his shirt, Eddie said, "One for the kill…" as he paused to cough up blood, "and one for the fun of it." He was daring Jack to take the kill shot.

Jack held his ground, silently. He didn't want to engage in any more conversation with this man. In the end, he shook his head, lowering the gun in the process. He had surveyed Eddie's wound and knew he had only moments to live. It wouldn't require him to sink to Eddie's murderous tactics.

Jack's calculation was right. Eddie's wheezing breath was soon extinguished for good and Jack let his arm fall back to his side.

He turned to look at Kate. She was on the verge of tears as she came running to him, her embrace nearly knocking him down in his weakened state. She cried on Jack's shoulder. He didn't know if they were tears of joy or tears of pain—probably both. He lifted his left arm to return the embrace, his gun hand still dangling as he struggled to feel anything as he looked down at the man who had caused him so much heartache. He figured he would be happy soon enough, but, if the truth be told, at that moment, he was exhausted.

"Come on, let's go," Jack said eventually. "Agent Travis is outside and he's hurt. He could use our help."

"And what about the money?" Kate asked as they stopped next to it.

After a short contemplation, Jack answered, "Leave it."

30

Jack and Kate saw daylight ahead as they walked together towards the mine entrance. Kate was holding Jack to keep him upright, but she found that it was him holding her together emotionally. She was relieved to know their ordeal was over for good but she hadn't stopped shaking yet. She felt cold and looked forward to being back in the warmth of the sun.

"Don't shoot," Jack yelled as they got close. "We're coming out."

They stepped slowly out of the mine, making sure Agent Travis knew it was them. Kate closed her eyes as she waited for them to adjust, tilting her head to the sun to soak in its rays. It reminded her how she felt the last time she had been inside a mine, and the relief when she finally got out. But this time she didn't swear off ever going back inside. This time came with a new sense of freedom that anything was possible.

"Nice to see you again, Miss Austin," Agent Travis said.

Kate turned to look, holding her hand over her eyes while still blinking. Although the brightness kept her eyes half-closed, she could see well enough to notice his white shirt saturated in blood around the shoulder.

"Agent Travis, you're bleeding," she said in reaction to the sight. Her instinct to help others immediately took over as she knelt down next to him.

He smiled and said, "You have what we call at the Bureau 'strong observational skills.' Have you ever thought about working for the FBI?"

She glanced at him with a confused look before realizing he was kidding.

"Glad to see the loss of blood didn't include you losing your sense of humor." she said back as she tended to his wound. She watched as Agent Travis shifted his gaze to Jack.

"I heard shots," Travis said hesitantly. "Did you get him?"

Jack nodded.

Agent Travis let out a deep sigh, before saying, "So it's over then." He holstered his firearm and asked, "And the money?"

"Inside," Jack said.

Kate watched as Agent Travis kept his eyes fixed on Jack, the silence lasting several seconds.

It was Kate who spoke next, saying what they were all thinking, "I guess you'll be needing statements from us about how we got the money then?" She continued to dab at Agent Travis's wound to make sure the bleeding had stopped.

Travis looked at Kate and answered solemnly, "That's how it usually works."

"I see," said Kate dejectedly. Her relief from the ordeal was not quite over after all, she thought.

"But you know," Travis continued. "I liked the first version of your story better…the one where you didn't take the money."

Kate was confused at first and suddenly realized what he was insinuating. She stopped dabbing to look at him, searching his eyes to make sure he was no longer joking. "Really?" she said as hope filled her eyes.

The corner of his mouth turned up into a vague smile. He looked around at the ground as he considered his footing. "Plus with all this loss of blood, it's hard for me to remember all the details anyway," he said as he started to get up.

Kate helped him to his feet. "But how will you explain us being here?" she said quizzically.

"You're the one that makes up reasons to come to the canyon. I'm sure you'll think of something to celebrate," Travis said.

Kate glanced to Jack. They did have something. She looked back to Agent Travis. "We have the best thing of all to celebrate. Jack proposed last night," she said beaming.

"Well, I hope you said yes. He's a good man," Agent Travis said looking at Jack with approval. "Now let's get what we need and go for some help. My wife is probably worried sick that I haven't called."

Agent Travis gave some instructions which included sending Jack back in to the mine to retrieve the money bags. When he returned, they all left together, making their way slowly back to the Hendricks land.

As they walked, Agent Travis made it clear that he had only interviewed them yesterday on the basis that he had a received a tip that robbers had used the old miners cabin as a hideout. When he went to investigate he met Jack who told him that he and Kate spent a lot of time in Green Canyon. His follow up interview with Kate concluded the same thing. They did, in fact, spend a lot of time in Green Canyon. Other than that, they didn't know anything.

Their appearance today was coincidental but lucky for Agent Travis, who had just finished off the last of the gang as he confronted them while they went to retrieve the money from the mine, the money the gang had hidden there. Jack and Kate had stumbled upon him during their hike and helped him back to where the road ended. Unfortunately, the gang must have shot Trigger while he was waiting back at the Hendricks land.

Once they arrived back at the road's end, they helped Agent Travis to a spot in the shade where he could rest. He groaned as they helped him down, but he was content to lay there in peace until help arrived. Jack had spotted some college students out for a hike awhile back and they immediately agreed to go for help. It wouldn't be long until the police and an ambulance showed up.

"We'll stay until help arrives" Kate said.

After a delay, Agent Travis replied. "No, you've done more than your share already. Why don't you two get going? Forget about all of this. It's time for you to move on with your lives. Go be happy."

Kate looked at Jack, his face somber with gratitude for the help and understanding of their new friend.

"You'll be a hero," Jack said to Agent Travis.

"Ok," he answered indifferently, still more human than hero. "Now go before I change my mind," he said to encourage them on their way.

Jack reached out and took Kate's hand. She followed Jack's lead as they began to walk away before stopping to look back. She couldn't leave knowing this might be the last time they see him.

"Agent Travis, will we ever see you again?" she said, her voice as humble and sincere as always.

Travis rolled his head towards them. "The next time you get kidnapped by bank robbers and are taken to a secret hideout in the woods, give me a call."

Kate watched as he glanced over again when she didn't respond to his joke.

"How about coming to our wedding?" she added.

"You just won't let me bleed to death in peace, will you?" he said sarcastically as he pondered his answer.

"Not until you say yes," Kate answered adamantly.

"Then yes," he replied, a smile creeping across his face.

Jack pulled at her hand and they were off.

As Jack and Kate walked out of the canyon, hand-in-hand, a string of emergency vehicles came thundering by them, the dust they stirred crawling over them in the process. After they passed, Kate noticed Jack had gone quiet. Looking like he had something on his mind, she asked, "What's the matter, Jack?"

Jack swallowed hard before he asked, "Did he hurt you?"

Kate understood the question. "No, you came just in time," Kate replied. "As soon as he heard your footsteps, and then your voice, he forgot all about me."

"Good," Jack said relieved. "That's good."

Kate smiled as she gave him a bump with her hip, "Believe me, it's more than good. I don't want to even imagine what would have happened if you didn't make it in time."

Jack smiled back, glad that she wasn't traumatized any more than she had been already. Somehow he had found a girl strong enough to stand up to the worst human kind could throw at her, and still return it with a smile and a joke.

"And how did you get over to that side of the mine to begin with? Didn't you remember the money was by the ventilation shaft?" Jack asked with a perplexed look.

"Yes, I remembered," Kate said as she walked slowly, letting go of Jack's hand to hold him by the arm. "But I kept thinking about what you said, how the money was the only thing keeping us alive, and I figured if I could stay alive as long as possible, that you might just save me yet, Jack Pepper."

"I think you ended up saving me," Jack replied.

Kate reached up to whisper in his ear, "I think we saved each other."

Jack stopped and turned to Kate, taking her in his arms, and said with a smile, "You know, that ear still hurts."

"Ok, how about this instead?" as she leaned in and kissed him on the lips.

"That hurts too, but I don't mind," Jack said, the warmth of her embrace pressing into him as she held him close.

"Come on, let's go home," she said, her house in view now.

As they walked in through the front door, arm-in-arm, Kate called out for her parents. They had done their best to clean themselves up, ready to explain another hair-raising adventure in the canyon by finding an injured FBI Agent, but there was no answer. The house was silent once again.

"Dad?" she called out. Still no response. She looked at her watch. "It's 2 p.m. on a Wednesday. No wonder he's not home," she said. "And I forgot my mother's still out of town. I guess we'll have to wait to tell them the good news," Kate said as she smiled. She watched as Jack formed a relieved smile.

Just then a small dog, still just a puppy, walked into the room and looked at them. Kate dropped to the floor and it came right up to her, never barking once. Soon after three more puppies just like the first, came to join them.

"Hi there little guys," Kate said as she played with them. "Did you miss me?" The puppies jumped up and around, on her and each other, making cute noises in the process. She looked up at Jack's face. He looked confused. "Jack, let me introduce you to the two sons and two daughters of our old friend, Trigger."

Jack's jaw dropped. He could immediately see the resemblance. He went and joined Kate at her side, petting the dogs as they sniffed and pawed at him. "I didn't know," he stuttered.

"Of course you didn't know. I hadn't had time to tell you yet," Kate said.

"How did this happen?" Jack asked, still in shock.

Kate raised an eyebrow in fun. "Sounds like we need to have a talk before our wedding night," she joked.

He smiled and gave her a playful shove. She grabbed his hand as he did and said, "Mrs. Judd, next door, has a beautiful yellow Labrador. Trigger instantly took a liking to her. We couldn't keep him out of her yard, the little devil. A few months later, these little guys came along. Mrs. Judd wanted nothing to do with them, of course, so I happily volunteered to take them," she said as she cuddled one up to her face to give it a kiss.

"So they're mutts," Jack said, thinking aloud.

"Yep, two proud heritages brought together to form one unlike any other. They're unique. That's why they're my favorite," Kate said, smiling proudly at Jack.

Jack was smiling too. Kate watched him as he got up, tugging at her hand for her to follow. They walked towards the front door.

"Where are we going?" Kate asked.

"If we are going to get married, you'll need a ring," he said.

"But Jack, we don't have any money…anymore," Kate said sarcastically.

"We'll stop by the bank then," Jack said.

"Didn't we just learn that robbing a bank is a bad idea?" she said playfully.

"I think they will give us the money if I ask nicely," Jack said.

Kate was now the one with a confused look, "Jack stop teasing. I don't need a ring right away. I have you. That's more than enough," she said.

Jack continued, "If I ask nicely, for the money in my account, from the sale of my father's property, I think they will give it to me. And it would be my great pleasure to buy you, Mrs. Pepper, a ring so the whole world knows you're mine."

Kate smiled, the tears starting up once again. She pulled Jack in to steal a kiss. A crime she would happily commit over and over again for the rest of their lives.

MORE ABOUT THE AUTHOR

For more information about Ryan Nelson, flip to the next page!

RYAN K. NELSON

2017 RONE AWARD FINALIST

2017 CHATELAINE BOOK AWARD SHORT LIST

Ryan released his debut novel, Cash Valley, in 2016. The suspense-thriller earned a spot as a finalist for a RONE award and made the Shortlist in the Chanticleer International Book Awards. In January 2018, Ryan released the sequel, Cash Valley: To Bring One Down. The second book has subsequently been nominated for both RONE and Whitney awards. In January 2019, the series finale, Cash Valley: An Unsafe Place, was released.

Read the full series and follow or friend Ryan on Goodreads.com

Made in the USA
Middletown, DE
24 October 2023